She Did It &

He Liked it!

COPYRIGHT

Edited by Hayzel Greene and Linda Taylor Fisher

Published by Hayzel Greene

Cover design by Hayzel Greene

Printed in the United States of America

DEDICATION

In loving memory of:

Willie Demetrius Jones "Bleu" – who opened my eyes to a world unfamiliar and allowed me to explore my mind's eye and write about it.

ACKNOWLEDGMENTS

Alhamdulillah.

All praises are due to Allah for granting me the ability to take the stories living in my mind and give them form on the page.

This book is dedicated to everyone who fuels me.

To my children—**Ty'Asha Le-She' Taylor (Alkhemist)** and **Raquiyyah Wakeelah Taylor George**—you are my why, my reason, and my greatest blessings.

To the man who knows me fully and still chooses patience and love—**Raymon George**.

To my foundation and stability—**Linda "Jeannie" Taylor Fisher**. To my father **Conway "Solomon" Fisher**, and my dad **Robert Leonard Farley**—thank you for your guidance, strength, and presence. To my brothers **Anthony "Butch" Meredith** and **Solomon Bey**. To my sister-cousin-friend **Angelique "Angel" Dupree Henderson (Hoop)** and my brother-in-law-cousin **Jody Henderson**—family in every sense of the word.

To my best friends—**Valerie "Val" Hopkins (Hommie Girl)**, **Dawn "Shy Sista" Haney Harnick**, and **April Mitchell Odom**—thank you for the laughter, honesty, and life support.

To my sisters from another mother—**Cheryl "Ms. Boo" Mott**, **India Scott**, and **Melisha Hawkins**—your love has never wavered.

To my soundboard and kindred sisters—**Tanya Nicole Anderson**, authoress of *Headturner*; **Marsha "Ocean" Lewis**, authoress of *G Spot Chronicles*; and **Kellie Brown**—thank you for the wisdom, encouragement, and fearless conversations.

To the **Varner, Wise, and Taylor clans**—your love reminds me that family is unconditional. I am proud to say I am **Taylor-made**. And to the **Fishers**—without your lineage, I would not be.

To my close friends—**Temujin "PNut" Hood** and **Willie Demetrius "Bleu" Jones (RIP)**—your impact remains.

To my **Kindred Book Club sisters**—Tanya Nicole Anderson, Patrice "Reesie" Avery, Kellie Brown, Diane Claiborne, Roynatta Mickens, and Nakita "Nikki" Lewis—thank you for the fellowship, the food, the laughter, and the conversations… especially the ones about books.

To my growth into womanhood, I thank my **Park Place One family**, the **HP Posse** representing Patrick Henry Junior High, Cleveland, Ohio, and my **Hay family** representing John Hay High, Cleveland, Ohio.

And to everyone I did not know that you are part of my journey, my growth, and my becoming.

TABLE OF CONTENTS

PROLOGUE

She Did It and He Liked It is a collection of ten interconnected short stories about choice, desire, and consequence.

These stories are not fantasies meant to excuse behavior or soften truth. They are moments—unfiltered and intentional—where women act first, feel deeply, and live with what follows. Sometimes pleasure is immediate. Sometimes it lingers. Sometimes it complicates everything.

Each story captures a different decision, a different risk, a different aftermath. Some are bold. Some are reckless. Some are tender. All are honest.

This collection centers women who are aware of their power—even when they misuse it, even when it surprises them. The men in these stories respond, react, pursue, or retreat—but the movement begins with her.

These are not love stories in the traditional sense. They are stories about agency. About intimacy chosen, not requested. About moments that don't ask for permission to exist.

This is where it all begins.

Chapter One
The Ride

Let me tell you about the day I had. It was one of those emotional roller-coaster type deals. By the end of the day, I was drained—physically and emotionally. It was so messed up, I didn't know whether I was coming or going. Some things I'm used to happenin', but when foolishness gets involved... that's when the shit hits the fan.

What I hate the most is when they throw it back up in my face. But what really puts the icing on the cake is hearing those four words: *"I told you so."* That sits at the top of my list of the worst things to hear when I'm already feeling fucked up for not heeding the warning signs.

Well, my *"I told you so"* came from the fact that my best friend, Brina, had no problem with her innuendos. In a lot of cases, when Brina spoke on a subject, she was typically right. In this situation, though, I had a hard time latching on to her persistent digs that my man—her cousin—was a cheater.

Of course, being in love, nose wide open, stuck-on-stupid, and nailed-down-shut prevented me from seeing the entire picture. I wouldn't have believed her even if she'd handed me all the cards from the *Clue* envelope—Miss Scarlet in the library with the candlestick. Shit... put your cards on the table. Show me. Put it in my face. Prove it to me—conclusively, without a shadow of a doubt—what the deal is.

Every opportunity she got, scenarios of him being unfaithful were drilled into my psyche. Damn, she was relentless with the hint-dropping and wisecracking. She would go on and on. One day, I had to tell her to shut the fuck up. I figured she kept talking because her ass was just jealous.

Besides, there were no telltale signs. No hard evidence. Generally, he stayed close by, so I could always put my hands on him. It was nothing for him to shower me with gifts. Financially, he could account for his money. Thanks to him, I got help with a bill or two, so that wasn't an issue. Mentally, he seldom seemed preoccupied; the man was on top of his game. Sexually… whew. The man had skills. I was satisfied in that area.

We hung out pretty frequently, so when did he even have the time? He had his place, I had mine. We had access to each other's spaces and could show up at any unexpected moment. I was pretty satisfied with our living arrangements.

Strangely enough, part of me was starting to suspect something might be going on after all. Even without concrete proof, it was beginning to make sense.

You know how you get that nagging thought lurking in the back of your mind? I'm talking about the one that lies dormant until something triggers something as simple as a car passing by, a word or phrase spoken, a scene, an action, or a combination of things. It's like a cousin to déjà vu or some'n.

I'd seen him texting and whispering low on calls. Can I say paranoid? Call it a woman's intuition, but when I really thought about it, a funny feeling hit the pit of my stomach. You'll never hear me say this out loud, but Brina may be onto something.

If he had another woman…, when did he find the time? I do know this: thirsty hoes get in where they fit in, sitting on the sidelines waiting for their turn to play. I say bench the bitches and keep it moving. Damn, now she got me second-guessing myself! Aww, her ass trippin'. Shit… he ain't fucking around. Better not be.

Most would wonder why Brina had such loyalty to me after all, he *is* her cousin. My explanation is this: first, she's a woman; second, she's my best friend; and last… then he's, her cousin. At least that's my order of operations.

We're thick as thieves, even though I don't always believe her. She tends to embellish—sometimes to get her point across. That's my girl, and I wouldn't have it any other way.

I must admit, at times I keep my guard up because sometimes, out of nowhere—*BAM*—right in my face, I get hit with another one of her shenanigans. Most of the time, I just laugh. But I *have* had conversations with her about her antics.

We had an agreement that, at least on our girls' day out, she would abstain from mentioning his name. Sure, we did things throughout the month, but once a month we made special plans. Oftentimes, she struggled with keeping our agreement—but she was strong-willed.

I discovered this place called It's Your Turn Day Spa, located just two blocks from the I-77 off-ramp. According to The Plain Dealer, it was rated five stars—an upscale spa with a price tag to match and excellent service. It would be well worth it. Not to mention, I owed it to myself.

The article didn't lie. The waiting room carried a safari theme, with lavender drifting through the air. Nature sounds floated from the speakers, instantly calming me. It was a far cry from my usual hip-hop and R&B.

"Hello, my name is Jocelyn. I'll be your host today."

"Hello," we responded in unison.

"How are you?" Jocelyn said. "I'd like to welcome you to It's Your Turn Day Spa."

"Fine—and you?"

"Your appointment doesn't start for a little while, but we have a tour of our facility scheduled. First, I'd like to say our purpose here is to satisfy our customers' needs as we take them to a world of ecstasy. Please follow me."

We stood, looked at each other, and gave a nod of approval, acting a little silly as we followed.

"According to our registry, you're scheduled for our Supreme Pamper Package, which includes a manicure, pedicure, deep tissue massage, and stone massage therapy. Excellent choice, if I may say. Hmm, let me see…" She scanned her iPad. "Your nail technicians will be Suzie and Juan. You have about an hour before that appointment, so let's get you prepped for your spa-cation."

She guided us to our private changing rooms. It was like walking into a bathroom straight out of *Architectural Digest*. The lockers were made of mahogany wood, each containing a white robe and shelves stacked neatly with towels. At the bottom of each locker sat a small safe, with signage instructing us to use the personal code provided during reservation. Now I understood why they asked for it—how ingenious.

There was a walk-in shower with waterfall showerheads hanging from the ceiling and along the sides. Sitting on the vanity were spa bathing products and a complimentary gift bag containing a bottle of body wash by Taylor Made Scentsations. A throw was draped across the bench, and resting on top was a spiral wrist keychain with the room key attached.

After undressing, I placed my valuables in the safe and jumped into the shower. They really had their customers in mind when they put this together.

After exiting the room, Jocelyn was waiting to escort me to the lounge area until it was time for our appointments. I could only assume Brina was experiencing something similar. When I arrived, she was already seated in an oversized chair, flipping through a magazine. I joined her, and we began discussing how pleasant the experience had been so far—and how much we were looking forward to the rest of the package.

During the conversation, the subject of men came up. At some point, I knew—without a doubt—it was killing her not to mention Dink. I could hear it in the tone of her voice. Usually, that's when things turn negative. Surprisingly, she held back. I realized that restraint was probably difficult for her, but she was doing well… so far.

I guess she was being merciful, allowing me to indulge in the moment—pampering my body and my mind. Believe it or not, she kept the peace. Talk about relief, I was glad she didn't go there. Then again, she might've just been distracted by the surroundings. Whatever.

Engrossed in our conversation, we didn't notice how fast the time flew. Jocelyn appeared at the entrance to escort us to our next stop.

"Ladies, food and drinks are on the house. Please follow me."

Talk about an oasis. This place was beautiful. One side of the room was a wall of windows stretching from floor to ceiling. Outside sat a large pool with several Jacuzzis scattered around it, surrounded by chaises and side tables. In the back was a bar with a circular waterfall backdrop. Greenery was everywhere—plants, flowers, trees—perfectly complementing the space.

Couldn't be in my house, though. Naw… that shit would probably be dead. A green thumb, I was not.

People around us looked relaxed and content. Some sat in groups, laughing and chatting. Couples whispered quietly in corners. If nothing else, there were free drinks to be enjoyed.

The mini-bar resembled the one near the pool—fully stocked. Everything from tea to wine, with an impressive selection of liquor behind the bar. In a refrigerated display sat fruits and salads.

"Ladies, what kind of refreshments would you like?" Jocelyn asked. "Today's special is Mimosa. It's one of our most popular drinks. Would you care for a glass?"

"Sure, that'll be fine," I replied.

"And you, ma'am?" she asked Brina.

"I'll have what she's having."

"I'll be right back."

"This is tight," Brina said. "Good service, comfortable atmosphere—we have to do this again. Soon. Real soon."

"Girl, did you see that pool? I wouldn't mind getting the gang together for a girls' day brunch. Remind me to ask about pricing before we leave."

Jocelyn returned with a cart. "Your Mimosas."

"Mmm… this is delicious. What's in it?"

"One part Champagne and one part citrus juice. We usually serve them during brunch or bridal events."

As she spoke, I noticed a man walking past the lounge—his body built to scream for attention, locs hanging down to his waist.

Whoa.

I nudged Brina with my foot. She followed my gaze.

"Damn," she said. "That man is fine."

Jocelyn glanced over and giggled. Closed mouths don't get fed.

She continued, pointing out the hors d'oeuvres—cream cheese blends, fruits drizzled with vinaigrette, jerk chicken coconut rolls.

"The Mimosa and hors d'oeuvres are complimentary. Would you like water as well?"

"Yes—can I get a glass of ice and a spoon?"

"Of course."

"This looks good as hell," Brina said.

"Please enjoy. I'll check back shortly."

"Damn," I said, lifting my glass. "This shit is good as fuck."

"Girl, you're going to be drunk before your massage."

"Maybe, maybe not—but there's enough for two more glasses in the decanter. We'll see," I said, pouring another. "And if your ass doesn't stop sippin' like a damn baby, I'm going to drink the rest and be extra nice. How about that?"

"Girl, give me a drink," Brina said, grabbing the decanter. "I can pour my own poison."

About a half hour later, Jocelyn returned—just as she promised.

"Ladies, how was everything?"

"It was perfect, thank you," I replied.

"I'm glad you enjoyed yourselves," she said. "It's time for your first appointment. Please, follow me."

She escorted us to the pedicure spa.

"Hello, I'm Suzie. I'll be doing your pedicure today," she said warmly. "Your unit is over here, ma'am," she added, gesturing toward Brina's chair. "Have a seat. Your operator is in the front and will be with you shortly."

Brina settled into her seat as Suzie prepared the station. I followed her lead, easing into the chair beside her and finally exhaling.

The pedicure spa was divided into six pods, each separated by patina metal partitions with Tiffany-style panels. The chairs were heated, elevated above the foot tubs, and paired with matching stools.

Lavender-scented water soaked my feet while Suzie worked her magic. The brown sugar scrub hit every pressure point. When she finished, my feet were smooth as a baby's ass. Period.

She painted my toes with the blue polish I selected, finishing with a custom design. By the time my manicure was complete, my hands and feet were silky smooth.

Johnny-on-the-spot, Jocelyn was there to take us to our next adventure.

"Your masseur awaits you. How was your experience? I gather everything went fine by the expressions on your faces," Jocelyn chuckled. "Come this way, please. The next part of your experience is the highlight of your package. I guarantee it."

We followed.

Shit, Jocelyn sho knows what to say. I got my mani and pedi done, and I'm ready for the rest.

When I walked into the room, there he stood, waiting to greet me… that is all I can say about that subject. What did I do to deserve all of this?

"Hello, my name is Malcolm. I'll be providing your massage today. Mickey, right?"

"Yeah, that'll be me," I responded jokingly.

"This way, please."

I looked back at Brina and winked. The expression on my face said it all. *Damn, this nigga is fine!* I don't know where they get them from, but these masseurs were built like brick shithouses—nice abs, nice asses, thunder thighs, and those arms. Mmm mmm mmm, I mean! I couldn't wait for Malcolm to lay those strong hands on me. Whoa.

A massage table sat center stage in the room. As I sat on it, I noticed a statue in the corner that had me doing a double-take. Shit, it reminded me of those fertility statues—the kind you see in cultural ceremonies with the big, erected dick. It felt almost ritualistic. Malcolm moved about the room like a Mandingo warrior.

"You're here for a deep tissue massage and stone massage therapy," he said. "Submerged in the bowl filled with light blue water are stones we call, in our business, Oriental basalt stones. I'll begin your massage by stroking your muscles with heated stones, then proceed to your deep tissue workout. If you experience discomfort or pain at any time, please let me know. Do you have any questions?"

"What did you say the stones were for?" I asked. I just needed something to say. Busy looking at him, I was listening—but not closely.

"I'll take the stones and massage your muscles. The heat helps relax them. Then I'll lay them on certain areas of your body—for example, along your spine."

I was a little geeked from drinking. The stones started looking like a bunch of bullets. The gleam reminded me of the silver of my ol' faithful. Just the thought of turning that baby on and sliding it inside me while it vibrated… I was starting to feel some type of way. The statue, the bullets, and this fine-ass man together equaled one hell of a good time.

"Are you ready to get started?"

"Yes," I said.

"I want you to remove your robe and lie on the table," he said, handing me a sheet.

I started untying my robe when he stopped me. "No, no—not right now."

"Oh, I'm sorry. I didn't know."

"No, that's all right—it happens frequently. I should've been more specific. Once you're situated, you can cover yourself with the sheet. I'll leave the room for about five minutes to give you time. Some people prefer to be completely disrobed, some partially—whatever you prefer is fine with me. Go ahead and get ready. I'll be back in five minutes."

I disrobed, lay on the table, and covered myself. When he returned, he assisted me in positioning my body as I placed my face in the cradle.

"I'm going to pull your sheet down some and start your therapy," Malcolm said. "Let me know if you feel any discomfort. Are you comfortable, Mickey?"

The minute his hands touched my body, I became aroused. "Shit... what I feel is horny," I mumbled.

"Excuse me—did you say something?"

"No."

Minutes into his deep tissue manipulation, I began drifting deeper and deeper into a trance as my subconscious conjured images of Malcolm nude. The imagery went to another level as I saw Malcolm transform into the statue I noticed when I entered the room. His dick was fully erected, like the Egyptian fertility god Min. Come to think about it, symbols of fertility were everywhere in the spa's design. Hieroglyphic wallpaper depicted Egyptians in all kinds of compromising sexual positions.

Malcolm slid his dick in as he rubbed the stones over my muscles. My entire body sprang into orgasmic bliss as he poured a blue liquid over me.

Drifting back into consciousness, I felt a warm sensation traveling down the middle of my back. Still in a haze, the feeling was so real I moaned and sighed as Malcolm strategically lined the stones along my spine.

"Is everything all right?" Malcolm asked.

I started laughing, playing it off. I explained that I was thinking about the scene where Martin Lawrence's costume started melting during a stone massage. If he only knew what really went down. I was about to lose it, thinking about the vision of his naked body on top of me, laying that dick.

"That *was* funny, wasn't it?" he chuckled.

Briefly, we laughed and talked. He didn't miss a beat. I guess talking was a distraction. I didn't mind, I was satisfied with the touch of his hands as he pressed and rubbed up and down my calves. The tightness in my legs began melting away. As he moved to my thighs, a tingling sensation shot straight toward my pussy. It was starting to feel like foreplay rather than a massage. I wasn't complaining—just saying. Naw, that shit felt really good. He had that magic touch.

Between him, the Mimosa, and the music, I drifted into a light slumber in no time flat. I must've slept for a minute—who knows how long—but I was well rested. Whatever he did, my muscle tone felt completely different. I hadn't realized how tense and stressed I was until now.

When I woke up, Malcolm was busy cleaning up.

"Oh, I'm sorry. I didn't mean to fall asleep on you."

"It's all right. You'd think people would stay awake during the manipulation, but some drift off. It happens. So—how was it, Mickey? I hope you found the massage satisfying."

"Veeeeerrrryyyy satisfying," I responded. "I really needed that. Thank you."

"I'm going to step out while you dress, and I'll be back in a second."

I sat up, taking a deep breath as I slipped on my robe. Malcolm couldn't have gone more than a minute when I heard a knock at the door.

"Mickey, can I come in? Are you decent?"

"Yes, come in," I said.

"Before you leave, I want you to drink a couple of glasses of water. It helps hydrate the body after a massage and speeds up circulation, since fluids are lost kind of like when you exercise. Jocelyn will make sure you get some."

"Thank you!"

"Here's my business card. Feel free to visit us again. My numbers on the back—I do parties and private massages on the side. Give me a call. It was great meeting you. Have a good day."

He extended his hand.

"I'll probably see you again—real soon."

No doubt, I knew I was going to try this at least once more, I thought, as I left the room.

Jocelyn escorted me to the Mantsopa Room, where I found Brina sipping on another Mimosa.

"You want some?"

"Naw, I'm good. I have to drive anyway. Malcolm said I should drink some water after my massage."

"OK!" Brina said, pouring the remainder into her glass. "Ohhh, Malcolm, huh? He said water—not wine. You better slow it up, talking about *me*!"

"Girrrrlll, I'm starving. You hungry?" I asked.

"Yeah, I could use something to eat. Then let's ride," she said, tipping up her glass.

We left, heading to our next destination—my favorite restaurant in the Flats.

"Did you enjoy your massage? I know I did."

"Girl, yeah—it was the bomb!" Brina replied. "I'm with you. We must do that again."

I've been going to Spaghetti Warehouse for well over two years—at least once a week. It was nice, quiet, and had a menu to die for. I'd been there so often I was on a first-name basis with the staff, and the chef knew exactly how I liked my food. I didn't need a menu because I ordered the same thing every single time. Funny thing is, whenever I went, the waitress still offered me one—just to see if I'd change my mind. I knew it was part of the job. So far, my appetite hasn't budged.

I always ordered my favorite: Wedding Soup and Veal Parmesan. Talking about moist and tender—the veal practically melted in my mouth. And don't get me started on that Tuscan tomato sauce. Straight fire.

We arrived, and as usual, the place was packed. We stopped at the bar to order drinks while waiting for our table. I still had a slight buzz from earlier, so I ordered something light. Even though several tables were available, I waited for my favorite one—not too close to the service door, but not too far from the restroom. Too much traffic distracted me, and besides, it gave me a perfect view of the entire restaurant.

Sam was walking toward the bar. "Brina, here comes Sam. Our table must be ready."

"Mickey, your table is ready. If you'd like, I can have your drinks delivered there. Are you ready?"

Still sipping, we waited for our appetizer and a basket of mouthwatering, freshly baked bread with butter. While I was talking to Brina—imitating Malcolm—I looked up and saw this chick talking to a waiter, dressed to kill.

"She is stomping the *fuck* out of those Louis Vuitton," I said, pointing in her direction. "Damn—when did they come out with that satchel?"

"Girl, stop pointing! Who? Where?" Brina asked, scanning the room.

"Over there by the window. Look—twelve o'clock."

"Damn, she's wearing *that* shit," Brina said. "Girl, I gotta get me some of those. Them bitches sharp as fuck—and that bag? Wow!"

"True dat—and she knows it by the way she's stomping to the motherfucking heavens," I said.

Although her outfit was to die for, today's events outweighed her paparazzi moment. We returned to discussing the day chitchatting about the fine-ass masseurs and how they worked our bodies.

"Just imagine if yo' man had hands like that," I said. "Girl, every night without failure, y'all would be fucking—and the foreplay would be those hands stroking that pussy. Talking about a damn appetizer while you wait for some head?" I chuckled. "Can we say bust one before he even gets started on the main course?"

"Girl, you know you silly—but yeah, I can imagine that" Brina said. We laughed so hard, tears started rolling.

"Girl, stop! Wait—hold up. Here comes Sam with the food."

"Your Wedding Soup, ma'am," Sam said. "Chicken and dumplings for you," she added, setting a bowl in front of Brina. "The rest of your order will be out shortly. Although I already know the answer—is there anything else I can get for you?" she asked jokingly.

That was a personal joke between us. She usually served me, and we'd built that kind of rapport. My response was simply to tell her to keep it coming as I dug in.

Halfway through the main course, the chatter in the room began to fade into the background. The restaurant was still full, people still talking—but the focus shifted to who had just walked through the door. The only sound I registered was the door closing.

In walked yours truly—Dink.

My first thought was, *how did he know I'd be here today?* I smiled—not a smile of pleasure, but more of a smirk. Confused. Something about seeing him here didn't feel right. Then I wondered, *Am I really that predictable?*

He looked around and headed in another direction. I wasn't sure if he'd seen me or not. I almost tried to get his attention, but something told me to wait. I watched to see where he was going.

He stopped at a woman's table.

She stood and hugged him.

It was her—the one sporting Louis Vuitton shoes and bag. She leaned in, aiming for his lips, but he pulled back slightly, turning his head. He resisted just enough—still letting her kiss him on the cheek.

"What the fuck?" I blurted out louder than I meant to.

Brina jumped. "What the fuck? What's wrong?"

Sam must've heard me because she came rushing over. "Is everything all right?"

"Yes—everything's fine. Just fine."

"You sure?" she asked. "I thought something happened."

"I'm sure. Everything's fine."

"Well, if you need anything, let me know," Sam said before walking away.

"Girl, what happened?" Brina asked.

"Girl, Dink just walked in, went to ole girl's table—and she kissed him."

"Where?" Brina said, twisting around. "Get the fuck outta here. What are you gonna do? I say whoop that ass and ask questions later. Better yet, let's fuck *both* of them up. I'll take ole girl, you take Dink."

I was fuming. Everything seemed to move in slow motion—except Dink and that bitch. I couldn't believe what I was seeing. Of all days and all places, why the fuck would he meet her *here*? My heart sank. I was crushed. I couldn't make a scene… or could I?

Contemplating my next move, I sat there and continued my meal. I wasn't even sure why I was going through the motions. I was on autopilot—eating simply because the food was in front of me and I needed something to do. The only thing I knew for certain was that I couldn't enjoy it. I was too distracted. I wanted to fuck him—and that bitch—up. Who in the hell did he think he was? And who in the fuck was *she* to him?

At the same time, I wanted to save face with Brina sitting there, watching me—waiting to see what I was going to do—with that *I told you so* look written all over her face.

Honestly, I didn't even want to know what the deal was between them. I was pissed and had adopted a full *fuck it* attitude. Call it denial if you want, but it was obvious they knew each other. They were far too comfortable showing that kind of affection in public. This wasn't their first time—they'd done this before.

What bothered me most was his body language. It was unclear. Why did he pull back? Why did he seem standoffish?

Slowly, the noise and chatter of the restaurant returned to the forefront. I could hear people talking again, servers shuffling around as they waited on customers. Dink and his bitch began blending back into the crowd. My mind started to resume some sense of normalcy.

Brina was saying something, but I wasn't really listening. Knowing her, it was probably a chant to whoop that trick. I tried to ignore the situation long enough to figure out my next move.

I wasn't ready for what happened next.

With her big-ass mouth, Brina did the unthinkable. She yelled loudly to get his attention. When he turned in our direction, along with a few other patrons, she motioned for him to come over.

"If your name ain't Dink, I ain't talking to y'all," Brina said.

"Brina!" I hissed. "Chill out—not so loud."

"Naw, that's some bullshit," she replied. "He knows what it is."

Dink hesitated. He probably knew he'd better come over before things got ugly. He knew Brina would set it off.

He started to excuse himself when Brina blurted, "Yeah—and bring *her* too!"

Knowing Brina, she either wanted to see ole girl up close or put her right in my face—one of the two. And he, like a dumbass, brought her over… or maybe she just accepted Brina's invitation.

As stunning as her outfit was, what stood out the most was the humongous rock on her finger.

That hurt even more.

My mind spiraled, imagining all kinds of shit. I was devastated.

When they reached the table, Brina spoke first. "Hey, Dink. What's up and who is this? How about introducing us to your girlfriend?"

"Yeah—who is this?" I added, my tone thick with sarcasm.

He looked stunned. I don't think he realized it was *me* sitting there with Brina until he got closer. He hesitated—not because of me, but because he knew his cousin. He was probably praying like hell that I wasn't the one sitting with her.

Wrong.

Brina is no stranger to getting her point across, and he knew she would've shown out if he hadn't come when she called. He was sweating bullets—and so was I. My body turned hot, clammy, and flustered all at once.

When she approached, she smiled wide and said, "Hi, my name is Sheila. I'm Darnell's girlfriend—soon-to-be fiancée."

"Darnell?" Brina and I said simultaneously.

"Your girlfriend? Fiancée?" I asked, locking my eyes on Dink. I swear, if looks could kill, his ass would've been toast. "How long has this been going on?" I asked, quickly turning my attention back to her.

Sheila answered immediately. "We've been dating for about six months. Today is a special day. I had some good news to share with my baby. My dad is going to make Dink a partner in our family business after we get married. We're opening an office in Cleveland Heights, and Darnell will head it. He's been talking about how this restaurant has some of the best spaghetti dishes in town, so I thought I'd break the news over lunch—before my dad let the cat out of the bag."

This bitch knew what was up. Don't no bitch give *that* much detailed information for no reason. Dink still looked stunned, like the cat had his tongue.

"My dad always thought Dink was the right one for me," she continued. "So, I picked out the most precious ring for myself and thought it would be nice for Darnell to see what daddy's money can buy. We needed to celebrate, and I thought this would be the perfect place."

"Proposal? Marriage?" I spoke. This bitch is crazy—she bought a ring! I couldn't believe this shit. Just the thought of him fucking around with this crazy-ass bitch had me hyperventilating.

"Yeah, marriage. How about that?" Brina chimed in smugly, staring straight at me. "I told you so."

Dink shot Brina a look that could've killed her on the spot.

"And *you* are?" Sheila asked.

"My name really isn't your concern," Brina replied. "But for the sake of keeping it real, my name is Sabrina. I'm his cousin. And the person you really should be concerned about is *this* lady right here. See, unlike me, if I had caught you kissing my man, I would've fucked both of y'all asses up. But Mickey? She's not like that. I've been trying to help her work on that for a while now, but she won't budge to save her life. Don't get it twisted, though—at the right time, she's a beast. So, you might want to step back behind him a little, because she looks like she's about to go for broke.

Brina could be condescending as hell, but this was one of those times when it was completely appropriate. She had my back, that's my girl.

"Oh… so *you* are Michelle," Sheila said casually. "He's mentioned your name on occasion. Now I can put a name to a face. I finally got to meet the infamous Michelle. I've seen your picture—he has a lot of them scattered around his office."

I stood up, using every ounce of restraint not to fuck this bitch up. "What the fuck you mean, what I look like?" I snapped. "So, if you knew about me, what the fuck is the problem?"

Brina stepped in front of me immediately. She knows I have a dark side—and that I will whoop a bitch's ass.

"Excuse me?" Sheila said, looking confused as she turned to Dink. "Dink!"

Still silent, Dink stood there motionless, his eyes darting from person to person as the tension escalated. He looked like he wanted to say something, his mouth hanging open—but before a word came out, I swung and clocked his ass.

He grabbed the side of his face, shock written all over him.

At that moment, I was done. Completely. The audacity of some people is unreal. This bitch knew about me and had the nerve to be so nonchalant about it. And him? Standing there stuck as fuck—caught, busted, and every other verb that described his sorry-ass situation. Leading her on or stringing me along… just what the fuck did he tell her?

By this time, all eyes were on me. Brina was smirking, Sam was approaching, and customers were fully tuned in to the show. Everything was happening so fast that I barely had time to think. Should I sit down and finish my meal—or should I leave? Better yet, should I punch his ass again and then whoop *her* ass?

The next move could make me or break me.

I'd already created a scene, so it was best to leave—avoid further embarrassment or, worse, catching a case over this dumb shit. I truly didn't want to be escorted out of my favorite restaurant.

Damn, this shit is fucked up, I thought as I signaled Sam over. "Sam, could you pack my food to go, please?"

"Yes, I'd be glad to," she said sheepishly. "Are you okay, Mickey?"

"No, I'm good. I'm good."

Dink and Sheila stood off to the side, looking like he was trying to explain something. I couldn't hear what was being said, but the tension was thick.

Fuck Dink. And shit—I'm glad I drove. Brina volunteered to take care of the bill. Sam returned with my food, and I grabbed my sweater, telling Brina I was out.

I brushed past him on my way out. As I reached the door, he came running after me, grabbed my arm, and swung me around. Why the fuck he thought that was a good idea, I'll never know. Instinct kicked in, and I swung—trying to punch the fuck out of him. He knew I meant business.

I rushed to my car, jumped in, and peeled off—*SKRRRR*—burning rubber as I merged into traffic.

I hit I-90, pushing seventy-five, eighty miles per hour. I was home in no time flat—and still fuming. My phone was blowing up, but I didn't answer a single call, including Brina's. I wasn't in the mood. All I could think about was what had just happened. How did such a perfect day turn into a damn nightmare?

Pinch me and wake me the fuck up, I thought. *This is some bullshit.*

I rushed into the house, stomach in knots, mad as hell. I kicked off my shoes and headed to the kitchen to put my food away. Who could eat after something like this? My heart was racing, blood pressure up—I needed to calm my ass down before I stroked out.

Let me get out of these clothes.

I headed upstairs, threw on my loungewear, then came back down. Once I started settling a little, a slight appetite crept back in. It felt like I'd just run a race. I tossed the food in the microwave to knock the chill off. Sleep wasn't happening—I'd had enough of that earlier—so I turned on the TV and flipped through channels.

Usher's *Climax* was on, one of my favorites. Normally, that would do it for me. Not today. I felt emotionally off kilter, stuck between sadness and betrayal. And that's when the tears came—pouring.

I closed my eyes and leaned back on the couch, replaying the restaurant scene repeatedly. My mind raced. Was there anything I could've done differently—not just today, but in our relationship—to avoid this bullshit?

Calm down, I told myself. *Stop. This shit is crazy.*

My phone lit up again. All three of Dink's numbers flashed across the screen. Ignored. I didn't have shit to say to him—I was done. Then a private number popped up.

I knew it was him.

Straight to voicemail.

How *dare* he? The audacity to call me after getting caught cheating. Thinking back, the signs were there—too many of them. Missing actions. Indiscretions. It was right in my face, and I still didn't see it.

A fiancée?

So, I'm not wifey material?

The devil really does work overtime.

I replayed all the things I *should've* said, *should've* done at the restaurant. Funny how that always happens after the fact. But as mad as I was, he better be glad I didn't leave his ass wearing the food I paid for—soup and all. Naw, that would've been a waste of my money *and* a good meal.

Yeah… this one caught me all the way off guard.

The microwave kept beeping. I got up, grabbed my food, sat back down on the couch, and started picking at it. Damn… this shit was still good. When I finished, I was too lazy to move, I left the dishes on the coffee table and stretched out on the couch.

Here I was, on my day off, hugging sofa pillows when I should've been hugging a man—*my* man.

Suddenly, there was banging on the door. I knew exactly who knocked like that.

Dink.

"Mickey, open the door, woman. Let me explain! I know you hear me—open up the damn door!"

Is he for real? I thought. *This nigga has got to be kidding.*

"Go away and leave me the fuck alone!" I yelled back. "Go fuck that bitch, Sheila! You better leave before I call the police!"

He came over here like nothing ever happened. The audacity. It wasn't that kind of party.

"Just give me a minute to explain!" Dink shouted. "Open the door!"

"Let him in, dammit, so he can stop all that damn noise!" Mr. Johnson yelled from next door.

I should've known his ass would be all in my business. Call him Ms. Bonita or Gladys Kravitz with his nosy ass—always sticking his nose where it doesn't belong. Mr. Johnson was the *last* person I wanted in my shit. He acted like a little bitch, always gossiping. This was right up his alley.

Let me answer this door.

I knew I was probably setting myself up. It went against my better judgment, but something inside me needed to know what was really going on. No—*I had* to know.

The moment I opened the door, he rushed in, grabbed me, and held me tight. Tears cascaded down my face. I was hurt, frustrated, and completely betrayed. Our emotions had been so intertwined—and now this.

No doubt, I loved Dink. He knew that. Everything about him turned me on. Sometimes he'd look at me with those seductive eyes, like he was staring straight into my soul. That shit was deep. And when we had sex? The pheromones coming off his body were intoxicating— especially when he wore my favorite cologne, Pi Type by Givenchy. It was like an aphrodisiac, a prelude to something even greater. He knew exactly what to do.

I hate to admit it, but I was weak.

Our relationship had grown to a place where sex was selfless. It wasn't just about getting off—it was about pleasing each other. That's why this shit hurt so bad. I truly believed I was *the* one. There shouldn't have been any need for him to be out fucking around on me. I gave him what he wanted, when he wanted it—and he kept coming back. This was supposed to be a two-way relationship… or at least, that's what I thought.

Hell, I should've let ole man Johnson call the police.

Dink clearly didn't appreciate what he had—because if he did, his ass wouldn't be cheating.

With his lips pressed to my ear and his breath heavy, Dink pleaded, "Baby, please… just let me explain."

I wasn't about to let him walk up in my house thinking everything was gravy—because it wasn't. I pushed him away, still pissed. The more he advanced, the harder it was to fight the feelings.

There we were, standing in my foyer, arguing over some bitch he was screwing. He paced, trying to explain, while I stayed on defense—doing everything I could not to let him have his way. I cussed and yelled while he tried to calm me down.

I hated it when he did that—tried to make it seem like *I* was the one out of control.

There he went again… manipulating me.

"Dink, why don't you just leave? You'd rather be with Sheila—then go be with her."

"Look, Mickey, if I wanted to be with Sheila, I wouldn't be here. Stop with that bullshit. You know I love you. I don't want that woman—she does nothing for me. Absolutely nothing."

"Huh. Bet you say that to all the girls."

"There you go. Shut up and listen," he snapped. "I don't want Sheila. That was all her idea. And that mess about her father thinking I was right for her, that was a damn lie. He knows I have a woman. As for her flashing her daddy's money, I make my own. I don't need her father's money. I earn what I make, and I do just fine for myself. You know that. And you need to stop listening to Brina. I love my cousin, but sometimes she doesn't know her place. She needs to stay out of my motherfuckin' business. I'm a grown-ass man. I saw how she was acting in that restaurant."

"Ain't nothing wrong with Brina! She's all right with me. She has my back—that's more than I can say for a lot of other people. And I *know*!"

Even though he'd nearly made his case, I struggled to hold my ground. He pulled me closer and kissed me. I was still trying to fight while his lips traced my neck.

"What about you dating her for—" I couldn't even finish the sentence.

"Shh. Hush," Dink whispered, tightening his embrace.

Who was I kidding? I gave in. I melted into his kisses and his arms. I thought I was fighting a good fight, but I was vulnerable. Good sex is how I got him, and I knew deep down it was what kept him. I knew what turned him on—and he never failed to satisfy my desires. Our sex life had always been *selfless*, meaning we never lost sight of pleasing each other.

Dink pulled me toward the bedroom. The shit was about to get real.

He was a freak in bed, and the freak in me was ready to come out. Before I knew it, I was lying down as he climbed on top of me. He caressed my earlobes, kissed my neck, and then our lips met. Listening to the low, soothing sound of his voice, my heart rate quickened, my breathing accelerating.

Dink was in rare form, coaxing us deeper into his lion's den. A fire ignited within me with every stroke of his hands along my inner thighs. I could feel my pussy opening, the wetness flowing freely. What started as resistance turned into full seduction, charged with passion. As we lay tangled in each other's egos, Dink's took control.

He stripped away my clothes. His muscular silhouette cast shadows against the wall as he rose to his knees, pulling off his shirt and tossing it to the floor. Watching him tower over me, lying there beneath him, fueled my anticipation for the powerful love he was about to lay on me. Dink was tight—his physique something to behold—and it made me want to surrender completely to his demands.

I'm not a sadistic type of lover, but there's something about a man's strength that heightens the experience. It's like a beast gets released—and once it's out, the sex is on and the beast takes over. A little hair pulling here, a little hair pulling there. A slap on the ass here, a slap on the ass there—nothing too harsh, just enough to keep the juices flowing. Sometimes I enjoy my sex hard and long. Sometimes I like it soft, but still long—it all depends.

He began caressing me as he removed my bra. As he sucked and massaged my nipples with his tongue, they became hard and erect. It's amazing how the nipples connect to other erogenous zones. While he sucked and flicked them, rhythmic signals radiated outward in all directions. My clit throbbed in anticipation, craving his touch with the same intensity. As he kissed my stomach, a rush of exhilaration surged through me and my pussy swelled.

Talking about ecstasy—when he finally hit my clit, it was out of this world. He gently licked, circled, and pressed with his tongue, sending waves of contractions through my clit and vagina. At times, he cupped my clit with his lips while manipulating it with his tongue. Intermittently, he massaged it—compressing, licking around it, then moving up and down. All I could do was lie there, gyrating slowly, round and round, up and down. The man knew how to give good head.

When his tongue hit certain erogenous spots, it felt like my pussy became electrified. *Whoosh*—the sensation spread and intensified as his tongue invaded my inner sanctum. My body responded with a burst of nectar as he stroked my clit. Dink was fully committed—must've tasted good—because he stepped his game up. While pleasuring my pussy, he grabbed my hips, lifted one of my legs over his shoulder, and worked my clit with pure finesse.

"Is this the way you like it? Is this how you want it?" he mumbled, his tongue circling and flicking my clit.

My body was in full ecstasy.

"Don't stop, baby. Suck that pussy—suck it," I urged, gyrating my hips. "This shit feels so good."

The sensations kept building, climbing higher toward climax—until Dink suddenly stopped and leaned back against the headboard.

Really?

He pulled me up onto my knees. I leaned in to kiss him, but he grabbed my hair, plunging his tongue into my mouth as he kissed me deeply, his hand still fondling my clit. Sweat dripped from both of us. He guided my hand to his dick, watching as I stroked him.

"Phew! Baby was that good for you?" he said. "Damn… that pussy was good. You should know by now I don't want anybody but you."

"You better not—because I know where you live," I replied.

"Come here, baby," Dink said, pushing my head down into his lap.

As I sat on the edge of the bed, he stood before me while I gave him head. "Suck that dick," he said.

As my tongue worked his shaft, I thought about the pleasure he'd given me. That thought alone turned me on even more. The freak in me agreed—his shit was the bomb. The act of giving oral sex heightened my arousal; my mouth became an erogenous zone as his shaft brushed against my lips.

Even though he denied needing other women, I felt compelled to show him that he already had the right one—and didn't need to look any further. I wasn't ready to let him go, not tonight. Tonight, I was cashing in all my chips. I knew I was crossing some of my own principles and that it was risky business putting myself out there like this. But there's something about makeup sex after a major fight that's undeniably intriguing.

The head was so good, I had him on his toes—moaning and groaning while I stroked his balls with my tongue. I was determined to fuck him so hard that anytime he thought of me, he'd flash back to this night. Hell, if the wind brushed against his dick, it would get hard just from the memory. Now *that* is what you call mad lovemaking.

Slowly, he gyrated back and forth, holding my head. Hearing his moans left no doubt in my mind that he loved the way I worked his dick with my tongue. The head wasn't just good for him—I was getting off on it too. My game had to be on point because satisfying my man mattered to me. And with my imagination running wild, the sex only intensified.

In my mind, I became a video vixen—a freak with legendary skills. The more excited he got, the harder he thrust forward as I jacked him off. I sucked faster, harder, knowing I had him right where I wanted him. His muscles tightened as he lifted slightly, letting out a deep sigh of pleasure.

"Damn, baby—what the fuck? Where did *that* come from?" he groaned. "Uh-uh… don't talk. Just suck that dick. Take daddy. Fuuuuccccckkkkk."

How scrumptious, I thought, locking my gaze onto my prey. My eyes traced his muscular body, and the look on his face sent chills down my spine. I knew I'd leveled up. As my tongue circled his head, the salty taste of his pre-cum spread across my mouth. When I swiped my tongue along his shaft, Dink shuddered in pure delight.

I know that hoe can't do this shit, I thought.

"Damn, baby," I moaned.

Caught up in the moment, he pushed me back, climbed over me, pulled my legs into a wide 'V,' and went back to work on my clit—kissing, licking, sucking it again. His movements grew more intense as his body started to tense. He buried his face deeper, working his tongue relentlessly while slipping his thumb into his mouth, then pressing it against me, slowly pushing further as he continued.

"Damn, baby—you taste good as fuck," he moaned.

"That shit feels good," I replied.

I could tell he was close. I kept stroking him, teasing his head, refusing to let him pull away. I gripped his thighs like my life depended on it.

"I'm about to cuuuuum," he said—and that was all the confirmation I needed.

He tried to hold it back, but with me driving stick, there was no stopping it. He let go, and I swallowed it all.

"Wow," he gasped, catching his breath.

He wiped the sweat from his face and collapsed beside me, satisfied. I rolled over, rested my head in his lap, and smiled to myself.

I was glad to be exactly where I was. What's-her-name didn't matter at that moment. She was a non-factor. He was mine—and I knew it.

"You done?" he asked.

"No," I replied. "You done?"

We were both trying to prove something to each other.

Still savoring the moment, we cuddled for a while, talking about the sex—some dirty talk, you know. Getting into a little afterplay, Dink asked, "Can you ride?"

"Mmm, I guess I can do that," I said jokingly. "Please, I thought you'd never ask!"

"Come here, girl," he said.

I straddled his body. As he held his dick, I lowered myself, guiding his head into my vagina. Pushing down further, I engulfed him, moving up and down, flexing my muscles around his dick. He grew more excited as I sank lower. Rising, he began pumping and gyrating his hips—fast, then slow—until he found a rhythm. That really turned him on.

Suddenly, he pulled me down onto his dick and blurted, "Baby, sit on Daddy's lap. Ride this dick for Daddy."

I grabbed a pillow, bending forward, crouched like a jockey on the back of a horse coming down the stretch.

"Damn, that feels good," he said. Holding my waist, he bounced and ground upward in rapid motions. "Ride that dick."

"How does that feel? Is this the way you like it, Daddy?"

"It feels good. Fuck me," I yelled, rolling and bouncing on his lap. Shiiiddd, I was doing my thang.

"Turn over—turn over," he said urgently. I lifted up and dropped to my knees. Ass up, face down. He slid his dick in and began moving around and around, in and out.

"Biiiitch," he muttered in pure pleasure. "This my pussy!"

Now he had the reins.

SMACK!

"Ride this dick!"

He fondled my clit. This was some crazy shit. Like I said, I wasn't really into sadistic stuff, but that slap on my ass felt good. With his dick deep in my pussy and his fingers working my clit, he blurted, "Shiiiit—who pussy is it?"

SMACK!

"It's yo' pussy, Daddy!"

Holding my waist, his body smacking against my ass, he worked it.

SMACK! "This my pussy. It's always gonna be my pussy, isn't it?"

"It's always gonna be yours," I said as I started to twerk on his dick.

Pumping and grinding harder and faster, he pushed toward climax. With one knee on the bed, he crawled forward, driving me toward the center. I felt him getting close, so I took control. He was helpless now—I had the reins.

"Ah, ah, ah—shit!" he cried out.

I ground, pulled, and yanked until my clit spasmed. He collapsed onto my back, going limp, breathing heavily.

"Damn, baby…" He kissed my forehead. "Man—phew!"

There's nothing like a good old G-spot orgasm. Completely satisfied, I lay in his arms. Wow.

Mmm, I needed that. After a fuck like that, I came back to my senses. Dink was wiped out—and I understood why. I worked his ass.

"Look, Mickey—about today, that's nothing you need to worry about. My love is right here with you. Remember that. I'll always be yours. And this dick right here"—he chuckled, pointing at his limp dick "will always be yours. Tonight, we did the De Bo Hagen and the De Grind."

He leaned in and kissed me.

He was exhausted. It wasn't long before he was knocked out. A few minutes later, my phone chirped. I rolled over, thinking it might be Brina checking on me.

Mmm… it wasn't Brina.

Whoa—it was Malcolm from the spa.

Damn, I forgot I'd texted him after all that fuckin' drama today. Mmm, he wanted to invite me out tomorrow. I'd deal with that later. Right now, I was too exhausted to even think.

Let me get my ass to sleep—got a busy day tomorrow.

I must be living right.

Chapter Two
The Set Up

"So now y'all got mutherfuckin' jokes in this bitch?" I snapped. "This shit ain't funny. Why the hell do y'all think I need y'all to hook me up? I don't need no damn help from y'all—or anybody else. Besides, y'all ain't got no taste anyway. These niggas burnt."

"But Ron is Joey's cousin," Shelly said.

"I don't give a fuck if he was Puffy's cousin," I replied. "That nigga got issues—and so do y'all if you think I would *evvvvvvvver.*"

"Girl, for someone who don't have a man, your ass sure in the hell is picky," Rachelle laughed.

"Don't worry about my picky ass. And you damn right I'm picky," I shot back. "If *you* were as picky, you wouldn't have fucked Trav when you were in the eleventh grade. Ugh!" I chuckled.

"Oh, so you throwin' low blows now? Fuck you, Lovey!" Rachelle snapped, waving her hand. "That nigga's curl was poppin', thank you very much. And anyway, I don't know what the fuck you talkin' about—his body was the shit. Besides, I wasn't the only one all over his ass in school. If memory serves me right, Shelly had the hots for him too. I just got lucky, that's all."

"First, that is *not* how I remember it," Shelly said, "and second, don't put me in y'all shit."

"And remember that nigga you hooked me up with last year?" I added. "You know—the forty-year-old rapper? He showed up to dinner with his jeans hanging off his ass. Really? Who does that? Oh wait—I guess *he* does. No thank you. You know what? I'll hook myself up from now on, so please—stop."

We looked at each other for a second… then broke out laughing.

"So my shit funny now, huh?" I warned. "Keep fucking with me and I'll show up to that wedding solo."

"You can't—you have to have someone walk with you down the aisle," Shelly blurted. "You gonna fuck it up."

"Pick somebody—*anybody*," Rachelle added. "It doesn't mean they have to be a date. Come on!"

"Phfft—changing the subject, Rach. I need to get that dress from you."

"Which dress?"

"You know—the chartreuse one. The one with the low neckline. And my earrings."

"Got a hot date, huh?" Rachelle teased.

"Nooo—company function," I replied.

"Don't tell me you're going by yourself," Shelly said.

"Unlike y'all bitches, I don't need a man to validate me," I boasted.

"You can't be serious—going all dressed up with no date," Rachelle said. "It ain't about validation. People do this kind of stuff."

"Yep—people do," I said. "And I'm gonna look real good doing it solo. Anyway, I plan to do a little mingling. Who knows what I might run into? Hell, boot camp did wonders for me." I turned around and smacked my ass. "On fleek. I'm gonna be all right. Like I said, I'm done with y'all hookups, a'ight? Let me get out of here—uh, Rach—"

"Your dress is in my bedroom closet," Rachelle said, "and the earrings are in the bathroom cabinet. You know where the spare key is."

"Well, ladies, I gotta go. Get wit'cha later."

When I pulled into Rach's driveway, every light in the house was on. Her bill had to be high as fuck if she burned lights like this when she wasn't even home. Shit—she's a baller; she can afford it.

I grabbed the key from its hiding spot and let myself in, calling out to see if anyone was home. No answer. I went upstairs to grab my dress and earrings. As I walked down the hall, I heard music coming from one of the bedrooms.

Rach hadn't mentioned anyone being there.

I figured it might be Stan, so I called out again—maybe he hadn't heard me the first time.

"Hello… is anybody here?"

Nothing.

"Hellooo?"

Still no response.

I moved down the hall more cautiously. If Stan was there, I didn't want to startle him.

"Stan? Is that you?"

I slowly pushed the bedroom door open and peeked inside to make sure the coast was clear. Damn—this bitch actually makes her bed every morning. When does she find the time?

Mmm… where is that dress?

Rach's walk-in closet was loaded. I hadn't seen half of this stuff before. She had some bad shit in here—shoes for days. With all these shoes, this bitch should be enrolled in Shoes Anonymous. Good thing we wear the same size. I need to come over more often and do a little shopping. Too bad she doesn't accept coupons.

Oh—there it is. Right where she said it would be.

I grabbed the dress and headed back toward my car.

Shit—I forgot the earrings.

Damn, I needed those. I turned back around. I set the dress over a chair and ran upstairs toward the bathroom. As I reached the hallway, I noticed steam rising from under the bathroom door.

Someone *was* home.

I was surprised I hadn't noticed before. I paused, looking down the hallway. I knew Rach hadn't come back—she would've said something. Lord, I hope that ain't Stan.

I need those earrings.

I tried one more time. As I approached, I saw the bathroom door was slightly ajar.

"Excuse me… Stan? Is that you in there?" I called softly. I tapped on the door. "It's me—Lovey."

No answer.

I pushed the door open slightly and peered inside. Steam filled the room—I could barely see anything. It felt like a damn sauna in there.

There was so much steam pouring out that I felt like an extra in the movie *The Fog*. Kind of creepy, huh? I could smell the scent of Issey Miyake in the air. Hell, I hoped I wasn't about to walk into some sinister shit where I die in the first five minutes. That would be fucked up, I thought, as I slowly pushed the door open.

I called out again, using my fake man voice, "Who's in there?"

"Me," someone responded.

It was a man's voice—but not Stan's. And judging by his silhouette, he appeared much taller than Stan anyway. Who in the hell could it be?

"Me," he repeated.

"Quit playing," I said. "I'm gonna call the police."

"Come and see who's in here," he replied.

Hell nah—this shit was getting *real* creepy. "Maybe I *should* call the police," I muttered.

"Naw, wait a minute," he said, peeking out from behind the shower curtain. "I knew it was you."

Knew it was me? This nigga has got to be kidding. I didn't even know him. But... looking like *that*, smart-ass mouth and all, he could get a pass.

The place didn't look disturbed when I came in—nothing broken, nothing out of place—so it had to be okay for him to be there. He must've been somebody. Maybe a guest. I'd never seen him before, but looking like *that*, I wouldn't mind getting to know that ass. Standing there naked, cool as a polar bear's toenails—he was confident as hell. With a body like that, he probably had every right to be.

"Me? You know me?" I said. "You must be mistaking me for someone else."

"No, I'm not," he said, continuing to rinse the soap from his body.

Everything was exposed—and I mean *everything*. Water cascaded down his body, and damn… he had a body to die for. When he finally shut off the water, he asked me for a towel, dripping from head to toe. The towel was well within his reach, but clearly, he was enjoying his little game.

So, of course, I handed him one.

Two can play that game.

I stepped back to give him room as he stepped out of the shower. If I could draw the perfect man, he would be it. The most beautiful bronzed complexion, sexy bowed legs, tight abs—muscular everywhere. His arms were as thick as my thighs. And baby… he was *holding*. Ooo-wee, was he ever.

Shit—if I didn't know any better, I would've thought I was in the wrong house. I definitely wasn't expecting anyone to be there. Rach never mentioned it.

"My name's Da'Ron. What's yours?" he asked, still drying off.

My, my, *my*—was I impressed. I hoped he didn't think I was being coy, but my face was flushed from seeing him standing there butt naked. Shy? I was not. And it was written all over my face. That man had an overpowering presence.

Why am I still standing here with my mouth open?

"I didn't catch your name," he said.

"Lovey," I replied. "My name is Lovey." Damn, I was fumbling all over my words, couldn't even get them out straight. "In a way, uh… I'm not sorry—but I *do* apologize for walking in on you."

"That's all right," he said casually, drying his legs. "I can't be a prude about it. Besides, you walking in was lucky for me—otherwise, I wouldn't have had anyone to help me dry off," he chuckled.

"What?" I shrieked.

"Whoa, whoa—I'm just playing," he said quickly. "Besides, you don't seem like the type of woman who goes for just anything from a man. Right?"

"Right," I said.

"Now that we've got that out of the way, just do me one small favor and dry my back."

"Really? You're kidding."

"No," he said. "Listen, I play a lot, but I would never disrespect a lady." He placed the towel in my hands.

Why is he playing these mind games? What the hell. There was no way I was passing up this opportunity. As I began drying his back, I couldn't help but notice how toned his ass was. I started at his shoulders and wiped downward to the small of his back. He had an ass like a stallion.

"I won't break—you can wipe harder than that. You missed a spot," he said, flexing the muscles in his back.

He had no idea. I'd already checked my shyness at the door. Yeah, I was a little rattled at first, but seeing him—trust and believe—I got my Mac on. When I finished drying his back, he turned around, took the towel, and tossed it over his shoulder.

Damn. Full-frontal exposure. What the *fuck*?

"Who are you again?" I asked.

"Da'Ron."

"No, I know your name. What I mean is—*who are you*? And why are you standing here butt naked in my girl's bathroom? I mean, I'm not complaining, but does she know you're here? She didn't mention anyone would be here."

"No, not really," he said casually as he applied deodorant. "She doesn't know I'm here—but it's okay."

"What do you mean, *not really*?" Hell, for all I knew he could've been a psycho killer with a nice-ass body. But he seemed normal enough. Still, here I was talking to a total stranger while he played mind games—and had me drying his back. Whatever the case, I was curious.

"I flew in early," he explained. "Rach wasn't expecting me for another day or two."

"Okay… so how did you get in?"

"Probably the same way you did—the key under the planter in the backyard. I'm comfortable saying that because if you didn't already know, we probably wouldn't be having this conversation."

"Okay, okay—I'll give you that," I said. "But you still haven't answered the question. Who are you? You clearly felt comfortable enough to be in here taking a shower."

"Her cousin," he replied nonchalantly.

"I know all her cousins—and I've never met you," I said. Over the years, she'd tried hooking me up with everybody between the ages of twelve and twenty. This one? I definitely hadn't met.

"Well, actually, I'm Stan's cousin," he clarified. "Which makes me her cousin by marriage—after they get married."

"Ohhh… okay. Stan's cousin," I said. "I might've heard your name mentioned before. Nice to finally meet you. Rach didn't tell me anything about you being here—I guess she had a lot on her mind." I glanced around. "Oh shit, what time is it? I need to run. Anyway, I'll let you get dressed. It was nice seeing you—uh, I mean, nice meeting you, Da'Ron."

"Yeah, nice meeting you too," he said. "Wait a second—let me throw something on so I can walk you to the door."

"Oh, don't bother—I'm good!"

As I headed down the stairs, I leaned against the wall. *Whew.* What the hell was *that?* By the time I reached my car, I was trying to figure out if I'd forgotten anything.

I had the dress…

Shit.

After all of *that*, I still forgot the damn earrings—the whole reason I went into the bathroom in the first place. Talking about a distraction… …believe this—and I know he won't either. Hell, I had to go back and get them—one of the main reasons I came in the first place. Huh. He was already on an ego trip, and I didn't want to inflate it any more than it already was. But I needed my earrings.

Fuck it—whatever.

As I opened the door, I hollered, "Da'Ron! Da'Ron! It's me again."

"Hey—back so soon?" he called out. "Come on in. Did you forget something… like a body massage, maybe?"

I played it off like I didn't hear that last part. "Well, actually, I did. I forgot my earrings."

"You didn't hear me, did you?" he said flirtatiously.

"Yes—I heard you. I was just ignoring you. I know how you like to play."

"Ah, come on. I don't bite," Da'Ron said, handing me a bottle of lotion. "Well… only if you don't want me to."

He stood there with his hand extended. I could've denied him, but instead I decided to see how far he'd go. I like a good challenge. I wondered what he'd do if I turned him down—probably try something else.

"What did you say your name was again?" he asked.

"Lovey."

"Nice to meet you again, Lovey."

After grabbing my earrings from the bathroom, I followed him into the guest bedroom, where he stood hanging clothes in the closet. By this point, I was intrigued. Da'Ron seemed intelligent—and he definitely came in a tight package. With all that going on, yeah… he had my attention.

Being in this room stirred up memories. I'd slept here many nights before, but tonight the room carried a whole new meaning—Da'Ron.

"Here—turn around," I said.

Instead of turning, he loosened his towel and lay on his stomach, shifting slightly to get comfortable. And trust—I could tell why.

I rubbed my hands together to warm the lotion. My intention was just to apply it—not give a full-body massage.

"How's this?" I asked as I began working the lotion into his shoulders.

Why did I do that?

It cracked Pandora's Box wide open. Even though I found him attractive, this was something I wasn't sure I was ready to open just yet. I was playing the game—not trying to win it. Because once you open that box, you never know what you'll find.

"You said your name is Lovey," he said.

"I distinctly remember telling you my name," I replied, continuing to rub his back.

He turned over, propped himself up on his elbows, and grinned. "I thought you said *lovely*—being pompous and describing your physical beauty," he laughed. "Rightfully so… you are lovely."

Oh—he was a smart ass.

"I don't need to compliment myself—that's corny," I said. "I'll leave that up to you."

I glanced at my watch and realized I was running *real* late messing around with him.

"Oh shit—I've got to go. Look, it's been a pleasure."

I gave his ass a few playful slaps. Before he could respond, I jumped up, rushed out of the room, down the stairs, and out the door. I could hear him calling after me as he scrambled toward the stairs.

"Hey—are you sure you—"

I was already gone.

As I jumped into my car, it hit me—I still had the key. I went back and slid it under the planter where it belonged. As I walked back to my car, he opened the door and called out, "I know you gotta go—but when will I see you again?"

"Soon," I said, pulling off.

Two days later, the girls and I met for lunch, chatting like usual.

"Lovey, got a date for you," Shelly said.

"Naw, I'm cool," I replied.

"The wedding is this weekend and you *still* don't have a date," Rachelle said.

"Like I said, I'm cool. I'll be there even if I have to go to Rent-A-Dick for the evening—I will," I said. "What's the number again?"

"Oh no, you didn't, bitch," Shelly snapped. "I've *never* had to rent a dick in my life. I can get a damn date, thank you very much."

"Stan's cousin, Da'Ron, is in town," Rachelle said. "I can hook y'all up. Trust me—you'll like him. He's right up your alley. Nice guy, smart, got vision. You know the type."

"Shit, I *know*," I said. "When I came over to get my stuff, I walked in on him… in your bathroom. I almost passed the fuck out. Talking about a body that won't wait."

"TMI," Rachelle said quickly.

"Didn't he tell you?" I asked.

"Girl—" Rachelle started.

"Do tell," Shelly urged.

"Girl, he stepped out of the shower holding about eleven inches," I said. "That one right there was holding for a couple people. You should've seen the dick on that man!"

"No—y'all bitches can talk about that shit *later*," Rachelle said.

"Bitch, don't think just because you're getting married you gotta stop talking about dick," I shot back. "Are you fucking kidding me? Talk about a bitch slobbin'."

"Again—TMI, bitches. *TMI*," Rachelle said. "I do *not* want to hear about my cousin-in-law's dick. How does that sound? The only dick I'm concerned about is *my* man's—not his cousin's or anybody else's. If that's all right with you!"

"Dick is dick," I said.

We laughed…

Later that night.

The phone rang around 11:30 p.m.

"Hello," I answered, my voice raspy like I'd just woken up. That was my *playoff voice*—the one I used when I didn't recognize the number or didn't feel like talking. I could've ignored it, but something told me it might be important.

"Lovey?" he said.

"Yeah—who is this?"

"Da'Ron."

"Ooookkkkaaaayyy…" I said, sitting up and clearing my throat. "Hey—how'd you get my number?"

"I asked for it," he replied. "Rach said if I wanted to know anything about you, I had to go straight to the source. So here I am. I had to beg and plead for it. Eventually, Stan gave it to me—so there you have it. That's how I got your number. I didn't think you'd mind."

"Well, it *is* kind of late," I said. "Hold on a minute."

I wasn't expecting a call so soon, but I figured I could talk for a minute.

"Da'Ron, are you still there?"

"Yeah, I'm here. Check this out—I need a date for the wedding. I wanted to know if you'd accompany me."

I noticed Rachelle hadn't said much about him at lunch. *When did all this happen?*

"Did Rach put you up to this?" I asked.

"Rachelle? No—she didn't," he said. "What makes you think that? And what does she have to do with me asking you? Wow—I didn't expect that reaction. Didn't you hear me say I asked her for your number?"

"If Rach had anything to do with this—no, I'm not interested."

"Why won't you go with me?" he asked. "Do you already have a date? If not, why not?"

"Are you *sure* she didn't put you up to this?" I pressed. "I told her—no more hookups."

"Hookups? I don't do hookups," he said. "Listen—she didn't put me up to anything. I asked for your number, that's it. I don't really know anyone here. Besides, I believe we're paired together in the wedding party anyway—so you're kind of stuck with me." He paused. "We might as well make it official. Hang out afterward—make it a date. And really, it shouldn't be a problem. You've already seen me in the most intimate way—naked. Doesn't that count for something?" he added with a soft chuckle.

"Yeah… I guess," I said, feeling a little conflicted. I *had* sworn I wouldn't let her hook me up again. But we'd see what happened.

"I'll take that as a yes," he said. "I'll see you tomorrow at rehearsal."

"Mm-hmm. See you tomorrow. Good night, Da'Ron. Talk to you later."

I hung up, still unsure how I felt about committing to a date with him. Past setups arranged by Rach always seemed jinxed.

On the other hand… Da'Ron. Wow.

Later that night, I opened my eyes to see him walking into my bedroom, naked—just as I remembered him from our first encounter. With his dick fully erect, I summoned him to join me in a blissful world of eroticism. As he crawled onto the bed, I aggressively pulled him toward me and straddled his body. My tongue traced a path to his sexy lips as my pussy pulsated with every tender kiss. In the heat of the moment, the cravings grew so intense that the only thing on my mind was embracing his body and getting my Jones off.

The thought of commanding him with my head game created a sense of dominance within me. Not in a dominatrix way—I don't seek erotic helplessness in my men, and I don't have sadomasochistic desires. Mine are sexual as well as mental. There was sanity in my madness. That pussy had the power to calm the virulent beast in a man. He needed to be a freak under the sheets, but ultimately, I wanted to feel that he was under my spell.

Watching him move closer, I began to salivate at the image of his dick in my mouth and his tongue working my clit. He rubbed the head of his dick between my legs, teasing my clit and occasionally pushing into my pussy. All I could do was lie there and let him play, feeling my body transform into a woman ready to conquer the beast. The sensation was titillating.

I wanted him—to ride him, to have him fuck me. His body was sculpted like a masterpiece, a true work of art. Without warning, he flipped me onto my back and began caressing my body. As he rolled my nipples between his fingertips, they hardened and stood at attention. With every lick of his tongue, an electrifying sensation shot straight to my clit. My pussy was wet with anticipation, my imagination running wild as I waited for him to finally push his dick inside me.

I was getting impatient. This foreplay was bullshit—I needed him to fuck me *now*. I didn't care how he did it, just as long as he put this damn fire out. From time to time, he used his fingers, sliding them in and out of my pussy until I was gushing cum like I couldn't believe. His miraculous hands found my G-spot in no time.

God, was he good. Manipulating my clit with his thumb while curling his finger deep inside me stole the show. He cupped my pussy as he stroked my clit, reaching inside to rub my G-spot, stroking and shaking me like a vibrator. Ripples of mild contractions built steadily, hovering on the edge of a climactic eruption. His rhythm was perfect—

moving from slow and gentle to fast and rough. At times, he applied just enough pressure to my clit with his thumb, sliding it from side to side.

The tension continued to build. All pleasure, no pain—he was a master of his art. It was as if he timed each stroke precisely, knowing exactly where to touch and when. My clit was so aroused I could feel the muscles twitching in sync.

Each time a mini orgasm hit, pleasure surged at my core, like I was steadily climbing toward a climax. My pussy spasmed as the contractions built higher and higher. I knew it was only a matter of time before I peaked. It felt as if an invisible string was being pulled tight in my crotch, and each pull sent a wave of pleasure through my body.

The faster he worked me—stroking and shaking—the more my clit began to twitch. A powerful tightening gripped my vagina as my body convulsed. That string was pulled taut. I froze as my pussy spasmed violently, the tension growing unbearable. The climax hit so hard I couldn't move. *Ahhh… oooo…* damn, that shit was good. As the convulsions slowed, my vaginal muscles gradually relaxed. The string finally snapped, releasing every ounce of tension in my body.

Da'Ron collapsed onto his back, breathing heavy and soaked in sweat, cum flowing from his dick. I snuggled in close, regaining my strength. We drifted into after-play—dirty talk, soft kisses—savoring the madness of the sex we'd just had. He stroked his dick while kissing me, and I touched myself, tracing his body and whispering in his ear. Before long, I noticed his dick hardening again.

As I kissed his chest, he pushed me onto my back and slid his dick into my pussy. I fuckin' melted. Rising up on his hands, he ground into me slow and steady, sending me straight into ecstasy. I lifted my legs and spread them wide so he could hit my walls, his body slamming against my clit, rubbing up and down, making sure I felt every inch of him. He played a wicked game of hide-and-seek—sliding all the way in, then pumping hard.

As our flesh met, the pace shifted. Our bodies moved in sync, grinding together in a steady rhythm. When he began to climax, his body spasmed as he thrust forward. Watching him come sent me into overdrive. I tightened my muscles and went full force as he yelled out. As his climax eased, I slowed my movements, riding out the moment until he finally collapsed, curling onto his side with me tucked in behind him.

Bzz. Bzz. Bzz.

The alarm blared. Damn—I needed to stay there just a little longer.

My panties were wet from my night with Da'Ron. I woke up feeling euphoric. If that man could do *that* to me in a dream… what the hell did he have in store for me in real life?

Yeah. I needed to find out.

We all met at Twill's, a high-end bistro on the Eastside, for the wedding rehearsal. I made it my mission to make sure I had his undivided attention. I went up in that bitch *popped*—hair and nails done, face beat to the Gods. My lipstick was tight, my lips inviting. That pimp-stripe, wide-leg pantsuit hugged every curve; I was *serving*.

We ran through the rehearsal without a single hiccup. Everybody was on cue.

During dinner, I sat next to him, brushing against him at every opportunity I could get. A touch here, a touch there—just enough to break the ice. Yes, we'd talked when we first met and even had some physical contact, but after *that* dream? I had other plans for Mr. Da'Ron.

I was starving, but I didn't really want to get my eat on in front of him. So I put on my best etiquette while eating. If I'd eaten to satisfy my *real* appetite, it wouldn't have been a pretty picture. Not that I'm a slob or anything—I just didn't want to look like I was famished, even though I was. Shit, I should've eaten before I came.

The room buzzed with chatter, but my focus stayed on Da'Ron. After dinner, our group lingered for cocktails. He was wrapped up in other conversations, but every now and then, he glanced my way with that sheepish smile—still playing with my mind.

I returned the look, pretending like I wasn't interested.

Right.

There was no doubt he had struck a chord in my curiosity. I wondered what was really behind those smiles and that body language. One thing was for sure—he was sexy. And two? I bet he could lay a good pipe. If not, I'd have no problem putting in some work and teaching that ass a thing or two.

But something told me he had plenty to offer. There was just something about his demeanor—I'd put money on it. If he was anything like the Da'Ron from my dream…

Tomorrow was going to be perfect.

In my mind's eye, I replayed flashbacks of my encounters with Da'Ron. It was like looking through a View-Master, clicking each scene one by one. *Click*—the shower scene. *Click*—his naked body. *Click*—spreading lotion over him. Each memory stirred deep emotions. The dream… whew. Just thinking about it had me hot.

The atmosphere was hyped—people hustling and bustling, getting ready for the wedding ceremony. Up to this point, Rachelle hadn't turned into a Bridezilla. I thought about helping the sistah out by slipping her a little *sumin' sumin'* from Shelly's flask. Leave it to Shelly to be holding. That probably would've calmed her ass down. On second thought, I passed. Rach just had to woman up—she's a big girl.

Time was moving fast. I still had to get dressed, but first I needed to paint her face and swoop her hair. She was a beautiful bride. Her dress was off-white—only noticeable if you were all up on it. We knew her ass wasn't a virgin. Oh, she tried to play it off, but we rode her ass about it. Wearing white wasn't fooling anybody. For real though, we didn't care—we were just fucking with her head. She bought the dress of her dreams, and that's all that mattered.

The men were dressed in black tuxedos with white shirts and apple-red ties and vests that complemented our gowns perfectly. They were exceptionally sharp. Stan's suit was tailored to fit, and Da'Ron… *phew*. All the bridesmaids lined up outside the doors, and the men joined us. As I glanced over at Da'Ron, I caught myself thinking that maybe a relationship wouldn't be such a bad idea.

When the organ music started, I snapped out of my daydream. As the doors opened, my heart fluttered. Hearing the Wedding March and feeling the excitement of my friend getting married made me a little sentimental. The room was filled to capacity—standing room only.

The officiant began his introduction, followed by the vows. He extended his hands between Rachelle and Stan and recited:

"Do you, Stan, take Rachelle to be your lawful wedded wife, to have and to hold from this day forward, for better or for worse, for richer or for poorer, in sickness and in health, to love and to cherish, until death do you part?"

"I do," Stan said, extending his left hand as Rachelle placed the ring on his finger.

Turning to Rach, Reverend Jones held her hand and recited:

"Do you, Rachelle, take Stan to be your lawful wedded husband, to have and to hold from this day forward, for better or for worse, for richer or for poorer, in sickness and in health, to love and to cherish, until death do you part?"

"I do," Rach said as she received her ring.

He placed their hands together and said, "With the power vested in me, I now pronounce you husband and wife. You may kiss the bride."

They kissed passionately. Everyone rose in ovation, celebrating their union.

It was official—I was the only one in the group without a man. *Let me not start a pity party.* It wasn't too late for me. In due time.

The photographer gathered us for bridal party pictures. Afterward, we moved to the reception room where the other guests had convened. By the time we got downstairs, the celebratory mood was in full effect—

laughter and chatter filled the room. A soft sonata played quietly until we were seated at the bridal table. The meals were served. We laughed, we cried, and we ate.

Da'Ron stood and tapped his glass, calling for attention as he gave the toast to the bride and groom. His speech was beautiful. One by one, we all took turns acknowledging their union—some heartfelt, some humorous.

The DJ announced the first dance. Stan and Rachelle looked stunning as they moved together to Luther Vandross's *"So Amazing,"* the perfect song for such a beautiful moment. Some guests sang along, tears and cheers blending as the couple danced.

I gazed over at Da'Ron as he sang along—he was really into it. The DJ kept the music flowing. When Al Green's *"Love and Happiness"* came on, the whole floor broke into line dancing. We *jammed.* There was R&B, reggae, rap—you name it, she had it. When that song ended, the DJ smacked me in the face with some old-school Babyface.

Da'Ron extended his hand and asked, "May I have this dance?"

"Sure," I said, heading back to the dance floor.

He started with his cheek pressed against mine, acting silly, whispering in my ear. Hand to hand, we Chicago-stepped to R. Kelly's *"Step in the Name of Love."* After all that dancing, I had to kick off my shoes. I think we danced to damn near every song— even a few I didn't like.

The night was beautiful, but all good things must come to an end. Rach broke tradition. Instead of tossing her bouquet, she threw the flowers that decorated the reception room to everyone—including the men—while Stan held the basket. It was awesome.

The limo arrived to whisk the newlyweds away. We gathered to see them off, then kept the celebration going. We danced, drank, and laughed until the wee hours of the morning. Eventually, Da'Ron asked to escort me home. Feeling a little tilted, I was down.

When we reached my door, I invited him in for a nightcap. Memories of how we first met flashed through my mind—him stepping out of the shower, beads of water glistening on his body. As fragments of the dream resurfaced, so did the erotic emotions tied to them. All night, we'd danced and flirted. There was no doubt he wanted the same thing I did.

We kissed fervently, his chest rising and falling against my breasts. I began stripping him of his clothes, and before I knew it, I was laid back on the couch. He hovered over me, cupped my breasts, kissing me gently. He helped me undress, then kissed his way down my stomach.

He spread my legs and positioned himself at my kitty. In a seductive voice, Da'Ron whispered, "Hi, my name is Da'Ron—nice to finally meet you." He murmured sweet nothings as he licked and sucked from the sweetness of my soul. "Mmm… this pussy tastes good. This is what I've been waiting on," he mumbled, kissing me again. He dove in, licking and sucking with increasing vigor. My juices flowed as he made sure not to miss a sip. The sensation intensified as he worked my clit with his tongue. It felt like forever since I'd had a man between my thighs—

especially one giving head like *that*. What a feeling. The licking and sucking carried me into pure bliss.

We moved to the bedroom, where he kept kissing me while fondling my clit. Things escalated. I grabbed a condom from the nightstand, ripped the wrapper with my teeth, and held the tip between my lips. I stroked him to full erection, then rolled the condom down his shaft with ease. After all that foreplay, I was ready for the main event. My pussy was slick from the stroking and sucking; sliding him in as I mounted him was effortless. His body shimmered with sweat as I bounced and ground on his dick. I closed my eyes and let the heat of the moment take over.

Nestled behind me, he slid in and began grinding slowly until he was all the way in—every bit of it, it seemed. He pumped back and forth, his pace and thrusts intensifying as he pounded away. I felt him getting close as his moans grew louder and he leaned into my back.

"Come to Mama," I said, excitement surging as I felt my own climax building. "Fuck me harder!"

I kept gyrating as his moans climbed. The louder he got, the harder I ground. Finally, he yelled, "Ohhh… ahhhh… shit!"

We climaxed together. The pleasurable pressure and tingling were unlike anything else on earth. Sex is one of the most gratifying sensations there is. Our bodies were drenched. The warmth of his skin was inviting as we cuddled. His strong arms wrapped around me, pulling me close, filling me with intimacy. I closed my eyes, cleared my mind, and listened to his breathing.

Snuggled in his arms, I thought about what a perfect ending it was to the night.

My girl got married—and I got laid.

The next morning, I woke to the smell of bacon. I got up and headed to the bathroom to freshen up. When I walked into the kitchen, he was standing there with nothing on but *my* apron.

Damn—*now* this is what I'm talking about.

I walked over and kissed him.

"Mmm, this is delicious," I said, sneaking a bite of his French toast.

"Here—sit down so I can feed my queen," Da'Ron said as he set the bacon on the table. "Last night was great. We definitely need to do that again. See what kind of service you get when you set it out? Breakfast on the table."

"It *was* great—and you got served," I shot back, laughing as we both cracked up.

We ate, talked, and spent a little more time playing around before he got dressed and headed out.

What an evening, I thought as I turned on the radio.

Well, I'll be damned—Luther.

Love has truly been good to me… Not even one sad day or minute since you came my way…

That's right. *So amazing.*

I couldn't believe it. But you know what? I could definitely get used to this.

A couple of weeks later, the girls and I reconvened our three-way calling ritual after Rach returned from her honeymoon. We talked about how the wedding and reception turned out to be the bomb, then pressed her for the lowdown on the honeymoon. Before revealing anything, she said she wanted to hear about *my* escapades with Da'Ron.

Ain't nothing to it, I thought. I was surprised she hadn't asked sooner.

"Girl, he fine as fuck—and not too bad between the sheets," I said.

"You nasty," Shelly laughed.

"Bitch, you do it too," I shot back. "It had been over six months, so you already know this pussy was good and hot."

"So… are y'all a couple now?" Rachelle asked.

"Can't call it," I replied, "but we've been spending a lot of time together. The sex is hot. I've been making up for lost time."

"He's cool people," Rach said. "I'm glad you're enjoying yourself. I know you were batting down all our hookups, so I stopped trying to hook you up. *Therefore…*" she paused, "…I set you up anyway, bitch."

"What the *fuck* do you mean?" I said.

"Well, when you told me you needed to come over to get the dress, I made sure Da'Ron was going to be there. I had no idea he'd be in the shower—but that was perfect timing," she said.

"I thought he said you didn't know he was there?"

"Stan told me he was coming into town," she explained. "He needed a date—and so did you. If I'd told you I wanted you to meet him, you would've been on some stupid shit—*I'm not interested, I don't need you to hook me up, blah blah motherfuckin' blah,*" she said, mocking me.

"So let me get this straight," I said. "Knowing all the other attempts failed, you decided to let me believe it was all my doing?"

"Something like that," she chuckled. "You mad? Stan said I shouldn't tell you."

"Did Da'Ron know about the setup?"

"No," she said. "Like I told you—it was just good timing on my part."

"So… are you upset?"

"Hell naw," I laughed. "That nigga fine as fuck, got a big-ass dick, *and* knows how to use it."

I danced around the room, snapping my fingers and singing,

"Love has truly been good to me…

So amazing to be loved…

I'd follow him to the moon in the sky above…"

Chapter Three
Cuddy Buddy

It was about time I opened this house up and let in some light and fresh air. Brush off the cobwebs, if you know what I mean, let my hair down and focus on *me*. It had been a long time since someone else's name came before mine. More like a little over a year since the last one flew the nest. I needed my space, and boy, was it hard convincing *them* that they needed their own space too. Now that my list was lighter, I could concentrate on what was next.

When you get to be my age, you start prioritizing things differently. Some folks call it a bucket list; others call it a New Year's resolution. Me? I call it Needs and Desires. If I put everything into perspective, I can usually tell what's really high on my list.

Everything feels important, but if I had to pick two, it would be renovating and dick. Not necessarily in that order—but definitely those two. It would be nice if they came simultaneously. It had been well over a year since I'd laid in a man's embrace and ended up with a good fuck. Shit, it didn't even have to be a *good* fuck. A lazy fuck and some good head would've been acceptable—just enough of one or a combination of both to bust a mind-blowing ass nut would've done me just fine.

Until I found the right one, I decided to stick to home improvement. I planned to open up Junior's room, expanding mine by adding a walk-in closet and an entertainment area. Ambitious, right? Thanks, HGTV. I figured I could live like I had money. I'd been saving for nearly two years, and if nothing unexpected popped up, I was good. Now I just needed someone skilled enough to carry out my vision. And hey—once the room was done, I could buy a new bed and break it in properly.

It took every bit of two weeks to clear the room for renovation. I went through just about every contractor list I could find, looking for someone reasonable with a solid portfolio and references. The interview process was grueling. I chose public places for meetings—just in case any weirdos applied.

After two hours of unsuccessful interviews, I sat with my head in my hand, regrouping before heading home. As I packed up to leave, a gentleman sitting behind me struck up a conversation.

"Sorry your applicants didn't work out," he said.

I was irritated from dealing with all the other losers, but I welcomed the distraction. "I was hoping I'd find at least one good candidate," I replied.

"Well, maybe you'll have better luck next time," he said.

"I hope so," I answered, standing to gather my things. "Take care and have a good day."

"Since your day went so poorly, how about I buy you a slice of pie and a cup of coffee?" he offered. "You do drink coffee, don't you?"

"Yeah—I drink coffee and eat pie," I chuckled under my breath. A refreshing conversation sounded good right about then.

He motioned for the waitress as I sat back down. It was clear he was job hunting—the classified section on the table was covered with circled listings. As the waitress approached, he slid the newspaper and pen aside.

"Ma'am, what would you like to order?" she asked.

"I'd like a glass of sweet tea with lemon juice, please. That'll be it—thank you."

"Sir, is there anything else I can get for you?" the waitress asked.

"No, I'm fine. Thanks."

"I hate lemon rinds in my drinks," I explained. "You never know what kind of bacteria is lurking."

He sipped on a Sprite he barely touched. Before I realized it, two hours had passed, and I was still sitting there running my mouth like I had nothing else to do. I genuinely enjoyed the conversation. I wasn't putting him on the couch—I'm no psychologist by any means—but I guess there's something about my energy that makes people feel comfortable opening up.

In that short amount of time, I learned a lot about him. He was easygoing, a good listener, and definitely a talker. For thirty-one, he came across pretty mature. What stood out most was that he'd recently served time for drug possession with intent to distribute. We weren't talking kingpin status—but he wasn't small time either.

Not only was he struggling to find work, but he also didn't have a stable place to live. He had some money stashed, but his bankroll was shrinking by the day. His past experiences had humbled him. He talked about regretting some of his life choices, about taking too much for granted when he was in the game. But what really struck me was when he spoke about the loneliness—being knocked down and forced to face reality while incarcerated.

I could relate to. The loneliness, anyway.

I heard his voice tremble when he mentioned missing one of the most important things in his life, not being able to see his son.

The conversation was getting deep. At times, it made me uneasy. With my bleeding-heart ass, I was listening to tragedy after tragedy and starting to feel sorry for him. That's one of my weaknesses—one I've been working on for a while. And that kind of weakness can get me into trouble.

"So… what kind of work do you do?" I asked, deliberately shifting the conversation.

Deflecting has always been my go-to defense mechanism whenever I feel myself drifting toward places I don't want to be emotionally.

"I dibble and dabble in this and that," he said.

"Humor me," I replied.

"Home improvement," he said. "I didn't just sit around while I was doing my bit. I took advantage of what was available and signed up for a home-improvement program. I promised myself I wasn't going back to prison."

He went on to explain how hard it was trying to go straight after being labeled an offender—especially coming from the lifestyle he lived. He talked about knowing too many career criminals and not wanting that future for himself.

"Yeah, I've been tempted to take the road of least resistance," he admitted. "But here I am. Anyway, enough about me. What about you? What do you have going on?"

I shared my renovation plans and why I wanted the work done now. When I finished, he outlined his qualifications and explained how he could help bring my vision to life. His approach wasn't aggressive, like someone desperate for work. In his line of business, you need a little more *oomph*—it's a dog-eat-dog world out there.

That was probably something he'd still need to work on.

Prison life might have taken some of that out of him. It's a different world now. I understood how that could be, though I also knew I could be wrong.

He offered to stop by and take a look at what needed to be done. Part of me was eager to get the project started, but another part of me felt a little anxious. His past gave me pause. I wondered whether he could really handle something this ambitious. But hell, the other interviews hadn't worked out. Maybe giving him a chance just might. If it didn't work out, I could always let him go.

I gave him my number and address and told him to stop by over the weekend to assess the job. We shook hands, and I headed out.

He rang my doorbell at exactly 9:00 a.m., ready to work. It was hot as hell that day. And he didn't make it any easier for me to stay objective wearing a wife beater, khaki cargo shorts, and a tool belt. His swag and that body caught me off guard. *Wow.*

I escorted him upstairs and walked him through my vision. He pulled out a pen, paper, and measuring tape and started jotting down specifications. We were on the same page. He was professional and clearly knew his craft. I was impressed.

"For this job, I'm going to need the following items," he said, rattling off a list of must-haves.

Luckily, I was prepared. I'd been planning this for a while—saving my money, buying supplies, talking to experts. I've learned that time is one of our most valuable commodities, and being punctual is important, especially when it comes to my home. I already had almost everything he needed to get started.

I just hoped this would work out.

"So, do you think this is something you can do?" I asked. "I've got most of what you need, and if anything, else comes up, we'll handle it as it goes."

"Yeah, I can knock this out in no time," he said. "When do you want me to start?"

"As soon as possible," I replied. "Let me know when you're available."

"I can start now if you want," he said. "We can talk contracts once I determine exactly what needs to be done. I'm reasonable—don't worry."

"Well, all right," I said. "Let's get started." I showed him the supplies I'd already gathered. "Before you get too far, though, we'll need to put a contract together—business, you know."

We agreed on reasonable terms, and just like that—it was on.

I gave him space so he could work. The heat was brutal. To make matters worse, the air-conditioning unit had to be removed so he could install a replacement window. When I walked back into the room, the heat hit me in the face. I was surprised he hadn't passed out.

The best I could do was grab the old industrial fan I'd bought from the hardware store. As I carried it upstairs, he stood at the top, wiping sweat from his forehead.

"Here let me help you with that," he said, meeting me halfway.

"Thank you," I said. "I figured this might help cool things down a little while you work. I don't know how you do it in this heat."

"This is nothing," he replied. "I work in heat like this all the time. But I appreciate it—thanks."

He went back to work while I found something else to do. I checked in on him a few times to see if he needed anything. With the temperature climbing and the humidity thick, I made sure he had something to eat along with a pitcher of sweet tea. I didn't want him to pass out from heat exhaustion.

Now that I think about it, him falling out wouldn't have been the worst thing—give him a little CPR, a little mouth-to-mouth, and feeling... I mean *pumping* his chest. Ain't nothing wrong with a little wishful thinking.

He stood there drenched in sweat, glistening from the sunlight pouring through the window. I handed him a glass of iced tea. As he took it, his fingers brushed mine, lingering just a second too long. There's something about the touch of a man's hot, sweaty hands that turns me on.

His thick frame was ripped. His belted pants rode low on his hips, fitting just right. The sight of his six-pack made me thirsty—in a very sexy way. And below that? He was hanging to the left. I mean, *holding*. If his dick looked that good through his pants, I could only imagine what it would look like exposed.

I had to catch myself from staring at his crotch while he talked. It had been so long that the sight of such a huge dick stirred feelings in places I hadn't felt in a while.

The first day was really productive—he got more done than I expected. Hot and sweaty, I figured I'd offer him the chance to shower. He accepted.

I adjusted the water temperature—another issue I'd been meaning to fix. I added it to the list; it would have to wait. There was still so much to be done. First things first.

I excused myself from grabbing some towels from the linen closet. When I turned back, I caught him standing there with the bathroom door slightly ajar—naked, his dick hanging nearly halfway down his thigh.

As I approached, I managed a quick, "Excuse me," handing him the towels. Meanwhile, my mind went into full sex-overdrive.

A year may not be long for some people, but it was long enough for me. Long enough that the sight of such a fine specimen of a man had me completely turned on. My pussy throbbed, sending signals through my body that *this* was right.

Damn, how I wanted to feel that dick inside me.

It would be nice if I could cross two things off my to-do list at the same damn time.

Damn.

That night, I thought about him most of the night, fantasizing about what I could do with that dick. Even though he was young, he definitely had it going on. I mean, he was hol-DING—emphasis on the *ding*. Like, his *ding-dong*.

I imagined how long and thick he would be with a full-blown hard-on. I daydreamed about all the positions we could try—smacking it up, flipping it up, and rubbing it down… Ohhh nooo!

Tempting as it may be, I needed to chill. He was young enough to be my son—well, a little older—but still. I kept reminding myself that there's nothing wrong with fantasizing. I hadn't acted on it.

Hell, he may be young, but he's a grown-ass man.

What am I doing?

After yesterday, my curiosity only intensified. Every chance I got, I found myself watching him as he worked—finding reasons to offer food or something to drink. It was a wonder the man got anything done with me hovering like that.

It was damn near obsessive, thinking about his fine ass.

I called my girl Tanya. I needed to talk to somebody. I guess you could call it *The Testimony of a Puma*. Some women are cool with the title *Cougar*, but not me. I prefer *Puma*. Same meaning—just hits different.

Tanya was that friend—the one I could trust with my most intimate secrets. The feeling was mutual. She was always my sounding board when life got heavy. That's how we rolled.

It had been a while since I'd experienced any real sexual release with a man. Talking it out was its own form of release—a way to process the tension. Sure, I'd handled myself just fine. Masturbation, toys, I got my Jones off. Then there was my Waterpik, what I called my *Water Dick*. Shower time became pleasure time, the water pulsing against my clit.

All that was cool… but it was missing the human touch.

I needed a man—plain and simple.

And right about now, I was stressed and horny as fuck over his young ass.

We laughed about it, but deep down I was serious as a heart attack. Tanya, with her analytical ass, helped me weigh the pros and cons like she always did. After talking it through, I decided I might test the waters a little.

She reminded me about the age difference and suggested I proceed with caution. What really stuck with me was when she asked what my expectations were, was I looking for something serious, or was this just lust?

That question made me pause.

I had to step back and really think about it. It wasn't simple, and I needed an honest answer before I could get my head right.

They say eyes are the windows to the soul. If that's true, then he *had* to know what was up. My eyes weren't hiding a damn thing, certainly not my body language. My attraction to him was written all over my face.

How could he miss it?

Watching him work felt like being at a sporting event, and I was his number one fan. I knew it wasn't appropriate to fuck the help—but damn, his body was undeniable.

Those bedroom eyes?

Mesmerizing.

If only I were bold enough to approach him—to build the nerve to seduce him for just one night. All I would need is one night with him to see what made him tick. I could already imagine giving him some head, feeling his sweaty body pressed against mine.

For some reason, I sensed there wasn't a naïve bone in his body, so giving me some head wouldn't be an issue. Only time would tell.

Damn, I needed to stop this madness. I'd been obsessed with this man since the day I met him.

The job was completed.

I was amazed by the results—it turned out even better than I'd anticipated. To show my appreciation, I cooked him a full-course meal. I wasn't sure when the last time he'd had one, but I was about to show him a few of my skills.

As usual, he ended his workday with a shower. By now, it had become routine for me to bring towels from the linen closet while he disrobed. He'd grown accustomed to my presence.

When I stepped into the bathroom with the towels, he seemed completely relaxed as he lathered up. Still moving with caution, I laid the towels on the stool and, on my way out, caught a glimpse of his body.

Damn, he looked good.

Something about watching him soap himself down turned me on. It would've been nice if it were me, he was touching—lathering me up instead.

"Dinner is almost ready," I said, closing the door.

We ate and talked about the job. Again—good conversation. Afterwards, he offered to clear the table and help with the dishes. Every time I turned around, I caught him staring.

I was flattered.

It was still early, and he didn't seem to be in any hurry to leave. I brought out a bottle of wine and put on a movie, though neither of us paid much attention to it. We sipped wine and kept talking.

Then, out of the blue, he said, "I know I'm young, but I must say… there's something about you that piques my curiosity."

"Really?" I asked.

"Yeah. And for some reason, I think you feel the same. You haven't said much, but I've noticed the way you've been watching me—while I work and while I'm in the shower," he said with a smirk.

"Really?" I asked again.

Damn. Can you say anything else but *really*? You're starting to sound like a broken record.

My heart was racing. This was it. What were you going to do? I'd known this moment was coming—and now it was here.

He turned toward me and asked, "Let me ask you a question, if I may?"

"Okay."

"What do you honestly think about me?" he asked. "Honestly."

"Honestly?" I repeated. "Well… I've had some thoughts. I've been curious—but I restrained myself. I didn't want to give you the wrong impression."

"What do you mean?" he asked. "Is it because of my age? Is that what's stopping you?"

"No," I said. "It's because you were working for me. And yeah—your age played a part. I'm almost old enough to be your mother."

The moment those words left my mouth, doubt crept in.

Old enough to be his mother.

"I see. Let me help you out here," he said. "Since I no longer work for you and you're no longer my employer, there are no business ties. Look, I'm a grown man—and I've been grown for a long time, trust me. I think you're a beautiful woman, not to mention a little funny at times. I like you. I like your style. So, what's the problem? Whether you know it or not, I see you've got mad passion about me too," he laughed. "And I hope you don't get the wrong impression, but I wouldn't mind making love to you—if that's all right with you. You've got flavor."

Before I could respond, he pulled me toward him and kissed me.

"Relax," he commanded.

I could feel his dick getting hard as our bodies pressed together. I thought about it, weighed my options, and decided it was all right—everything about it felt right. The rationalizing was over.

Over the past few days, he had shown a level of maturity that was refreshing—more than some of the older men I'd dealt with. I wasn't here to take advantage of him. He was a grown man; I could clearly see that. Like any opportunist, when they see an opportunity, they take it. This was an opportunity—one I had thought through.

So, I took it.

"Okay… I thought you'd never ask," I managed to say.

It felt like my world was opening up to something new and exciting.

He grabbed my hand and led me toward the stairs. Things escalated quickly as the foreplay intensified. He seemed more excited than I was. Before we even made it upstairs, clothes were everywhere; shoes here, blouse there, shirt here, bra there. By the time we reached the top, there was a trail leading from the living room straight to the bedroom.

Once we crossed the threshold, he backed me against the doorframe, kissing me deeply while his hands roamed my body. I was so caught up in his kiss that my heart rate skyrocketed. I was hot.

Pulling away from the frame, I backed toward the bed, dragging him with me.

Lying on the bed, he began kissing my thighs slowly, deliberately. As I ran my hands over his head, he moved to my most precious possession, caressing my clit with lingering kisses and then attacking it with sudden, ravaging strokes. It had been a long time since I'd had head this good.

I was on the verge of losing my mind as his tongue flicked and pressed against my clit. My entire pussy throbbed. Then I felt something brush against the opening of my vagina a different sensation altogether.

"Wow… what's that?" I asked softly.

Without a word, he lifted his head, revealing a tongue ring.

Damn.

Who would've thought a tongue ring could add that much intensity? I'd never had head from anyone with a tongue ring before—how would I have known? That wasn't even on my list. Let me add it… and scratch it off.

He worked it expertly, gently holding my clit between his teeth while stroking it with the tip of his tongue. The sensation was so intense that he had me inching toward the headboard. It was almost too much to bear—my clit convulsed, my stomach tightened, and my thighs trembled.

He restrained my legs as I gripped the sheets.

He engulfed every essence of my sacred treasure, something I'd been missing for far too long. I twisted, twerked, jerked, and finally cried out, "What are you doing to me?"

He was locked incompletely in the zone.

I cleared my mind and let the sensations take over.

As he continued his magnificent performance, there was nothing I could do but cum.

I lay there exhausted as he slowed his pace, taking one last lingering suck before releasing me. My juices flowed like nothing I'd ever experienced before. I had to give him credit—this was way beyond my expectations.

He lifted himself onto his elbows and licked me, trying to catch everything I was giving him. Some of my cum slipped past his reach and ran down toward my ass. He lifted my leg and made sure he caught it all.

Damn.

He was a freak—and no joke.

And I loved it.

He grabbed a towel from the nightstand and wiped his face.

"You good?" he asked.

Before I could answer, he said, "It's my turn."

Standing at the foot of the bed, he guided my body toward him and began kissing my breasts, sucking my nipples while remaining upright. Feeling elated, I lay back with my eyes closed, visualizing his fuck game. When he crawled between my legs, I shivered with delight, anticipation flooding my body. I had been fantasizing about him putting his dick in me—and now here it was.

He Inserted the head, rotating It around the mouth of my pussy like a whirlpool spinning in the middle of the sea. Slowly, deliberately, he pushed further, inch by inch, hips rotating with control. When I asked for more, he gave me the whole enchilada.

"Is this what you want, baby?" he asked. "Is this how you like it?"

He was smooth—easy with it.

Leaning in, he whispered, "Are you feeling me?"

I felt him sliding in and out, grinding deep, his shaft hitting and rubbing the mouth of my pussy. As he worked that dick, I gasped for air, my voice completely gone. There was no denying it—this man was a man. I felt alive. And I didn't want this to end anytime soon.

All that built-up testosterone gave him stamina. His pace picked up as he pounded my pussy, switching positions effortlessly, turning the sex into one of the best encounters I'd had in a long time. The man had muscle—real strength. He held me in positions I never imagined my body could handle.

At one point, I lay on my back with his dick in me, my legs closed together underneath him as he pumped. Then we shifted into a scissor position—him at one end of the bed, me at the other—our legs intertwined, his dick buried deep while my clit stayed pressed against his body. We held onto each other's legs, grinding hard and heavy. The more we zoned in, the closer I felt the climax creeping up.

The grinding intensified. The pumping grew faster, harder. The bed rocked beneath us. And just like the rhythm of the grind, we came hard—together.

But the sex wasn't over.

There was a brief reprieve. We talked—about sex, about random things—hands still roaming, bodies still connected. Before long, we were right back at it.

Damn... this man had longevity.

Switch.

He laid me on my back, crossed my legs, and pushed them toward my head. Sliding inside, he braced his arms and stared directly into my eyes through my crossed legs as he began to grind.

Switch.

Rising to his knees, he pulled me into his body and thrust himself inside me again. It was on. He picked up the momentum, fucking me faster, harder.

"Keep going," I said breathlessly. "I'm about to cum. Ooo... that feels so good."

Fucking like a jackrabbit, my clit began to twitch, my vagina contracting uncontrollably. He hit the right spot, and a volley of contractions rippled through my body.

"Ah... ah... ah... ooo," he moaned.

There's something contagious about that moment right before climax. As I reached my peak, it was like my body gave him permission to let go. Coming at the same time created the perfect orgasm.

I came hard—strong—yelling his name louder than I did when he was giving me head. I fucked him with finesse.

He will remember my name.

Talk about putting it on him, I did that.

Or did he do me?

Either way, even though I'm the older one, I won't take all the credit.

Because I must admit… that man had game.

Well, even though I'm the older one, I won't take all the credit. I must say, he had game. Besides, come to think about it, I'm probably not his first puma. No muss, no fuss—he was doing too much. Whew! That man knew how to hit that thang. He was a keeper.

We lay in each other's arms, enjoying the quiet comfort of one another until we drifted off to sleep. Later, I felt him get up and heard running water. Too exhausted from my workout to move, I felt the warmth of a washcloth as he gently wiped my face, my neck, and between my legs.

How thoughtful was that?

When he finished, he lay back down, cuddled me close, and fell asleep.

I woke later with his arm wrapped around my waist. Carefully, I moved it so I wouldn't wake him and slipped into the shower. I was sure he was exhausted from the morning's festivities. After showering, I went downstairs to prepare breakfast.

You know the sex is good when you wake up feeling exhilarated.

Just thinking about him sent a warm sensation through my entire body—talking about a full-body orgasm. Yeah, that's exactly what it was. My body was glowing. This young man had it going on across the board. Shit, I needed to stop referring to him as a boy. He wasn't a boy, he was young, yes—but not a boy by any stretch of imagination.

Just as I was setting breakfast on the table, my thoughts were interrupted by a knock at the door.

Who is it? I thought, slightly aggravated. Of all times, somebody had to be at my damn door.

"Who is it?" I asked as I approached.

They said something, but I couldn't quite make it out.

"Who is it?"

"Tanya!"

Shit… I forgot she was supposed to pick me up.

"Hey girl, wait a minute!"

Damn, I wasn't even dressed—and there was no way I was leaving with him still here. No way.

Opening the door, I said, "Girl, it completely slipped my mind that we were supposed to hook up today. I'm sorry. Come on in," giving her a hug as I invited her inside. "Come into the kitchen while I finish up."

"What's up with you?" she said, eyeing me. "You look a little different this morning. Is that a glow I see?" Tanya teased.

"Girl, let me tell you—last night was off the chain. I finally got some dick," I told her.

"Get the fuck outta here!"

"So yeah, last night? It was on," I said.

"The young guy…?" she asked, eyebrows raised.

"Well, he didn't fuck like he was young," I replied. "That dick was awesome. And don't let me forget to tell you about the head game. Damn—he had skills to pay the bills up in this muthafucka! Can I get a hallelujah?"

"Well, good for you," she laughed. "I'm glad you finally got some dick in your life. So… what time did he leave?"

"Leave?" I spoke. "Wait—girl, let me tell you something. He knocked me straight the fuck out. When he washed me up afterward, I could barely move."

"Washed you up?" she said. "Damn! Can you bottle some of that shit?"

"No, my sista—you gotta get your own," I said, imitating the man from the Lifetime commercial.

"So when can I meet him?" she asked excitedly, taking a seat.

"He's upstairs, sleep."

As soon as the words left my lips, he came down the stairs—slow and steady—thick, muscular calves on display. Polo boxers hugging him just right, dick on swole. Just the thought had me salivating for that body.

He didn't realize I had company.

Before I could stop him, he blurted out,

"I woke up dick hard and hungry, thinking about that thick, juicy pussy and how you put it on me. I want you for breakfast—so jump up on the island and spread your legs so I can eat."

As he rounded the corner of the staircase, Tanya stood up, turned around, and froze—mouth wide open in pure amazement.

With a stunned expression on his face, scrambling to cover himself, he yelled,

"Ma!"

Chapter Four

Dare

It is not often that you develop a friendship like the one I share with my girls. We met on the first day of kindergarten, grouped together by our last names. What a coincidence—not only were our last names close alphabetically, but we were compatible in every way that mattered.

Our relationship grew over the years as we shared the highs and lows of life, which only brought us closer. You name it—we've done it. Friends for life. That's how we saw it, and that's how it remains.

By the time we reached sixth grade, times had changed, people had changed, and our innocence had changed too. It was Sam—yep, she started it all—with Danielle's dare to steal from Mr. Wilson's store. And of course, she did it. I was too outdone, but just like the rest of us, I ate the evidence. Laughing, thinking she had just pulled off the slickest move ever, we made a pact never to tell anyone about our dares.

We agreed we would never steal again—but other dares? Those were still fair game whenever the urge struck.

After high school, we headed off to separate colleges, taking us not only to different geographic locations but down very different paths in life. Still, we talked weekly, keeping each other updated on everything going on. Sam had recently graduated with a bachelor's degree in Pharmaceutical Medicine, and to celebrate, we planned a trip to Vegas.

None of us had ever been there before, and we wanted to see if it really lived up to its reputation as Sin City.

We stayed at the luxurious Luxor Hotel, and the rooms were nothing short of magnificent. We were booked in the Pyramid Suites, decorated with Egyptian furnishings and offering a panoramic view of Las Vegas. My room was Suite 304—symbolic to me, since that's my birthday. I chose it thinking maybe it would bring me good luck.

Something good was about to happen. I could feel it.

We were in awe. It had been a long time since we were all together like this.

Since we never really laid our dares to rest, I figured it wouldn't hurt to stir up a little excitement. After all, we were here to celebrate Sam's graduation—what better way than with a dare?

Sam was up for the challenge.

Our rule was simple: each dare had to re-enact a scene from a favorite movie.

Sam went first. She jumped into a water fountain and re-enacted a scene from *Under the Tuscan Sun*. People gathered around watching her perform, probably thinking she was part of the entertainment. That shit was hilarious.

Danielle was next. Somehow—because she's always been resourceful—she got her hands on a maid's uniform. Her dare was to re-enact *Maid in Manhattan*. She took pictures playing dress-up in someone else's clothes.

Now that was risky.

Not only did her ass get a maid's uniform, but she also got hold of a master key card. She got away with it, but the scary part was realizing how easy it had been. If she could get one, who else could?

Both of their dares were successful.

Now it was my turn.

I chose *Crazy, Stupid Love*. My dare was simple—but bold: pick up, seduce, and fuck some unsuspecting man. And no, it couldn't be just any man. I had preferences, so I set the agenda.

All dares had to be completed before the trip was over. Our flights left the next day, and I hadn't even started.

Each dare had to include a real element of risk—something that pushed the edge. After Sam's fountain scene and Danielle's maid impersonation, I knew I had to go all out.

Success was only part of the thrill.

Talking about it afterward—that was where the real excitement lived. The adrenaline rush didn't end with the dare; it lingered long after.

As we gathered at the bar on our last night, Danielle and Sam shared their experiences. We laughed about how they both managed to pull off their roles without getting caught. Then Danielle asked the million-dollar question.

"Dana, how's your dare coming along? You know you don't have much time left, right?"

"Yeah, yeah, I know," I said. "I'm working on some things. It'll be completed by the end of the night. I've got time. Mmm… how about another drink? Waiter!"

It was time to step my game up and handle my business. My dare was to pick up a man, seduce him, and fuck him. It wasn't that I was procrastinating — the ones I'd come across just didn't meet my stipulations.

Danielle and Sam had successfully completed their dares, so I had something to prove. The clock was ticking, and I knew my deadline was closing in. Still, I wasn't sweating it. Vegas is a big city — something was bound to give eventually.

We sat around reminiscing and catching up until I spotted him walking toward the bar.

That's the one.

Booyah.

He was alone — a definite plus. I just hoped he wasn't in Vegas with someone, because that would throw a wrench in my whole plan. Before he sat down, I caught a glimpse of his face.

Not bad. Not bad at all.

From the back, though? Even better. Broad shoulders, long locs — yeah, he was definitely checking boxes. He fit the criteria. He had to be attractive; that was non-negotiable. Another requirement? He had to be well-endowed. Small dick energy was a no for me. I needed to *feel* it.

And let's not forget head. I'd dealt with men who could do one or the other, but finding someone who could handle both? That was like beating the odds in the casino.

Alright. Here we go.

I stood up, adjusted my clothes, downed a shot for courage, and got ready to go in for the kill.

"Watch me work," I boasted, popping a mint into my mouth as I headed toward the bar.

Damn — he looked even better up close. This was about to be easy.

Tapping his shoulder, I said, "Excuse me, is anyone sitting here?"

"No, you're good," he replied, gesturing for me to take the seat.

Mmm. I like this already.

"What's your name?" he asked.

"Dana. My name is Dana — and yours?" I said, shaking his hand.

"Antwon."

"Nice to meet you, Antwon," I said, giving him a nod.

Tilting his head slightly with a mischievous smile, he asked, "So what brings you to Sin City?"

"Celebrating with my girls," I said, pointing back toward Sam and Danielle. "What about you?"

"One of my bruhs is getting married tomorrow. A bunch of us came out here to send him off in style."

"Ohhh, a bachelor party," I said. "Hope y'all having fun. Is it one of those drinking, naked hoes, making-it-rain, rites-of-passage kind of situations?"

"Yeah, something like that—but it's cool for a minute," he said. "I got tired of all the noise and hoes shaking all over my drink, so I had to take a little break."

"Well, I don't want to disturb your peace. I get it when you want to be alone," I said as I stood up. "I hope you enjoy the party, though."

Please stop me, I thought.

"I said break, not solitude," he replied. "Are you turning in for the night? If not, stick around."

Bam. He took the bait. It was on and popping.

"No," I said casually. "I think I'm going to grab some coffee and a little something to eat. It's been a while since I last ate, and I'm feeling it after getting my drink on. I probably should put something on my stomach."

"Can I join you?" he asked.

"Sure. Let me take these drinks over and let my friends know I'm out. I'll be right back."

Whoa—talking about tilted. Standing up after that last drink had me a little tipsy. I considered asking the bartender to deliver the drinks, but figured I could manage. Besides, I wanted the girls to know I was about to hit the jackpot if things went the way I planned.

I carefully balanced the drinks, hoping I wouldn't stumble and embarrass myself. After setting them down, I glanced back to see if he was watching.

He was.

"Look what I found—about to hit the lotto up in this motherfucka' tonight!" I laughed. "Don't have time for chit-chat. Later, hoes—I'll get wit'cha!"

Of course, they flipped me off, laughing as I walked away toward the bar.

"Night, ladies," I said.

"Well damn," Sam said. "Isn't that the pot calling the kettle black?"

"Be careful—and have fun," Danielle added.

Antwon and I headed over to the Pyramid Café for a late-night snack and coffee. We sat, talked, drank coffee, and ate. Not only was he a fine specimen of a man, but he was also intelligent.

Like most men I've met, he was dealing with personal issues that needed sorting out. The saying *you can't judge a book by its cover* rang true. Everyone needs an ear—and I guess tonight, it was my turn.

I learned a lot more about the man beneath the surface than I had intended. I reminded myself: *I'm here to complete my dare.*

He had a bachelor's degree in Criminal Justice and was working toward a law degree. He came from a family of lawyers. Sounds like he had it all together, right?

The problem was pressure—his father pushing him to keep the family tradition alive. Becoming an attorney wasn't his first choice. He talked about the constant arguments, about his father trying to control his life instead of recognizing that he was a grown man capable of making his own decisions.

What bothered him most was being threatened with financial cutoff from a trust fund that had been promised to him.

As he unpacked all his drama, I found myself offering suggestions. Almost—*almost*—feeling sorry for him.

Damn. That wasn't part of the plan.

One side of his dilemma was staying in his father's good graces and continuing life as a silver-spoon baby if he followed the legal path. The other side was choosing his own dream and risking regret if he didn't.

We spent time tossing around possibilities. I suggested maybe there was a way to do both—honor his father's wishes *and* follow his passion. More importantly, I told him that whatever choice he made had to be one he could live with.

Who wants to be denied their dream?

The conversation was good, but time was slipping away. I realized I didn't have much room to play, so I knew it was time to cut to the chase. I didn't want to come off heartless, but I did become more direct.

"Listen, if you're truly unhappy, you should pursue your dream," I advised. "That doesn't mean becoming a lawyer is a bad idea, though. If you think about it, once you pass the bar, you'll always have something to fall back on if you need it."

I could tell he appreciated my input. Something in his expression shifted, like the fog had lifted just a bit. Then again, I thought to myself—hell, what do I know? He'll figure it out.

We talked for another hour. The clock kept ticking, and I knew I needed to get this show on the road. Glancing at my watch, I finally said, "I think I'm going to call it a night. It's been a pleasure meeting you, but I need some rest. I'm leaving tomorrow. I'll probably just watch a little TV until I fall asleep."

I was betting the odds would fall in my favor—but you never know. It was a risk I had to take to complete my dare. I'd made my move; now the ball was in his court.

"Can I walk you to your room?" he asked, signaling for the waiter. "Would you take this, please?" He handed over his credit card, then signed the receipt when it returned.

"You sure? I don't want to inconvenience you," I said. "I hope your friends aren't wondering where you disappeared to."

"No, I insist," he replied. "Trust me, they're fine. Chances are they've probably passed out by now. It's no problem—I'll walk with you."

I'm no mind reader, but I've always considered myself a pretty good judge of character. Most of the time I'm right—though I've missed the mark more than once. Nobody's perfect.

We were probably thinking the same thing.

I was still playing the odds, and so far, they'd been in my favor. Some famous gambler once said, *"The best throw of the dice is to throw them away."* Right now, that felt painfully relatable.

My plan hadn't fully come together yet, but the good news was—I still had another roll of the dice. The difference between us was simple: I wasn't here trying to fuck on a dare… well, actually, I was. He, on the other hand, was likely thinking about fucking because that's what some men do when they're single, lonely, or unattached.

Then again—single or not—some men aren't serious about the relationships they're already in. In Sin City, at a bachelor party? Please. He was definitely potential.

We never discussed commitments. But honestly, that wasn't important. This was a dare.

And either way, the night was shaping up to be interesting.

When we reached my suite, I invited him in for a nightcap. Things were unfolding smoothly—almost too smoothly. I started to wonder whose plan this really was.

Digging through my purse for the key card, I finally opened the door. Before stepping inside, I kissed my fingers and tapped the **304** on the doorplate for good luck.

At that moment, it wasn't about luck anymore.

It was about a good fuck.

"What was that?" he asked.

"Oh, just glad to be back in my room, that's all. Come on in and make yourself comfortable," I said as I opened the drapes.

"May I turn on the TV?" he asked.

"Sure, help yourself," I replied. "Make yourself comfortable."

As I glanced out the window, taking in the landscape below, I saw the scene differently than before. Earlier, I'd been too focused on getting my party on to truly appreciate the view. The lights glowed, the gold glittered, and the ambiance was everything.

So this is Sin City, I thought. *What happens in Las Vegas stays in Las Vegas.*

Who had time to watch television?

"Antwon, excuse me while I slip into something more comfortable," I said.

"Sure—go right ahead. Hurry back."

I returned wearing a baby-blue robe that hugged every curve like it had been tailored just for me. That got his attention. He sat up straight, eyes wide.

We talked about how the evening started. He had me cracking up about the bachelor party—especially the part where one of his friend's women showed up unexpectedly. I knew that had to be a shock.

Even though I was enjoying myself, I stayed mindful of the time, waiting for the right moment to make my move. Timing was everything. I didn't want to come off like I was rushing him out—no, not at all. I wanted *him* to make the first move.

Still, not wanting to leave it to chance, the words slipped out.

"Well, it's getting late, and I've got a busy day tomorrow. I really had a wonderful evening."

As I reached for the door handle, he grabbed my hand. His fingers slid through my hair as he gently stroked my cheek. Then, in the heat of the moment, he leaned in and kissed me—something I'd been planning all night.

Bingo.

Almost there.

The wait was worth it. If he fucked like he kissed, I was in good shape.

Our tongues danced in sync, sending waves through me like ripples across water. He slid my robe down off my shoulders, massaging them as he kissed my breasts. I flushed instantly—juices flowing. When I glanced down and saw the bulge in his pants, I knew exactly what was coming next.

The man had a dick on him.

Lying back on the bed with him hovering over me, he kissed me slowly, sensually. He worked his way down, nibbling at my breasts as my clit continued to swell. His tongue traced my stomach, tickling me, making me flinch at the spots that were suddenly extra sensitive.

Funny how every touch became more intense the closer he got to my pussy—*Queen Clit.*

He helped me out of my panties while I touched myself. Lifting my legs, spreading me open, he went straight to my clit. He covered my pussy with his mouth, sucking like an algae eater stuck to aquarium glass—lips everywhere.

Flicking. Sucking. Alternating with precision.

His head was so good it had me squirming, pushing at him—though I couldn't go far. He had me pinned down, locked in, moaning and grabbing for anything within reach while he shook his head side to side.

Nothing was breaking his rhythm.

That shit was *good.*

"What are you doing to me?" I gasped.

"Making you cum," he mumbled. "I know what you need."

No, shit, Sherlock, I thought. I wasn't ready for him to stop. I wanted to hold on to that feeling as long as I could. He was doing just fine.

Latching onto my clit one more time, his lips engulfed it firmly. He shook his head again until my pussy started contracting and my clit twitched, swollen and hard. Everything was so sensitive that wherever he placed his tongue, I trembled.

"Damn, baby, you like that, huh?" he said.

Barely able to speak, "Uh-huh," I managed.

Coming up for air, he said, "Cum for me."

Oh my goodness, this shit feels good.

He started stroking his dick as I watched, playing with myself—fingers sliding in and out, round and round. He sucked his thumb, then slowly rubbed my clit before pushing it inside my pussy, shaking it rapidly and steadily.

As I gyrated, my vagina began to tighten and contract. When I tensed up, he talked me down, calming me with his steady voice. He kept fingering me, rubbing my clit—sometimes jockeying for control. Our constant motion pushed me to the edge.

Within minutes, I was about to cum for this stranger I'd brought into my world.

"I'm cumming... ahhhh," I moaned.

"Come on," he said. "Give me that pussy."

The pleasure was so intense it had me humming and moaning. Whatever he was doing to me, it was powerful.

"Are you okay?" he asked, standing up and wiping his face with the backs of his hands.

"Whew... I'm fine."

"This is just the beginning of what I have in store for you," he said.

I propped myself up on my elbows and watched in amazement as he kept his rhythm, jacking his dick, pre-cum glistening. When I say he was holding, that was an understatement. My pussy pulsed with anticipation. I didn't know if I could handle something that big—but I was game.

I reached for my phone on the nightstand and snapped a picture.

"Why did you do that?" he asked.

"I had to make sure that when I wake up in the morning, I have proof you weren't a mirage," I replied.

He chuckled and kept going.

Standing there naked, his thick, heavy dick stood fully erect. He pulled a condom from his pants pocket and rolled it on—had to be a Magnum, as big as he was. The look he gave me said he was ready to do some serious fucking.

This ride was going to be a challenge, but we'd come too far to stop now.

He crawled between my legs, stroking himself before guiding the tip inside me. My pussy stretched to capacity. Propping himself on his hands, he rocked back and forth, inching deeper as I rolled my hips in slow circles, helping my body open up for him.

My mind drifted from his thickness to how good it felt filling me. The more he worked it, the wetter I got—and the better it fit. Once past the head, it was smooth sailing. He was all the way in.

The longer he fucked me, the more my body adjusted, flexing and massaging his dick from the inside.

Once he knew I was comfortable, he started switching positions. First, he lifted my legs onto his shoulders and settled back onto his heels.

That one took me to school.

Shit.

Two hours later, we were still fucking.

Fuck it… this is a dare. I'm going all in.

If I can't walk tomorrow, I'll crawl to the front desk and ask for a damn wheelchair. That's how good it was. It's not like I'll ever see him again.

I backed away from him and dropped onto all fours. He stretched across the bed, positioning his head between my legs. He licked and sucked my clit while I stayed on my knees, occasionally slipping his tongue inside my pussy. I gyrated and grinded, zoning out under his steady manipulation.

The shit was so good I nearly smothered him, sitting right on his face. The man knew exactly what he was doing.

Afterward, he pulled himself up and dragged me back to the edge of the bed, taking me from behind. He slid that big dick into my pussy and started slow and easy, rolling his hips. As he picked up rhythm, he slapped my ass in time with his strokes.

I could tell he was getting close — faster, harder, deeper. At one point, I had to brace myself with one foot on the floor because he was humping with everything he had. He was fully zoned.

"Baby, you like this dick?" he asked. "I said, is this how you like your dick?"

"Ooo, baby, yes," I moaned. "Fuck that pussy. You like this pussy? Show me you like this pussy."

He was right there. When he started to climax, he crawled up onto the bed, pulling me with him. I collapsed under his weight, face down, ass up, his dick still buried inside me. I kept gyrating while he yelled and moaned, his body jerking as he finally came.

When he rolled onto his back and slipped out of me, it felt damn near satisfying watching it end. I've never been so excited for a nigga to cum. He fucked the absolute shit out of me — and I loved every second of it.

We passed out afterward.

It felt like only five minutes had gone by when the phone rang. Danielle. I reached for it quietly, careful not to wake him, and moved toward the foot of the bed.

"I'm okay," I whispered before hanging up.

When I looked back, his six-foot, dark, chiseled body shifted as he reached across the bed, searching for me. His dick lay soft against his thigh.

"You alright?" he asked.

I smiled. "I'm fine."

He rolled over and hugged the pillow. "Excuse me — I need to use the little girl's room."

As I stood, my legs nearly buckled. Weak in the knees. What the fuck did he do to me?

I steadied myself and made my way to the bathroom, closing the door behind me. I dialed Danielle and Sam on three-way while running the bathwater.

"Oh my fucking God," I whispered.

"That good, huh?" Danielle laughed.

"Good is a fucking understatement," I said. "I'll fill y'all in at breakfast, in the cab, at the airport — whenever."

"Damn, bitch, that's a long-ass tale," Sam chuckled.

"Yeah," I said, laughing. "Big-ass dick with a side of Deeze Nuts," before hanging up.

Carefully stepping into the tub, I draped a warm towel over my eyes. Reality set in — my time was running short. I washed slowly, my body sore.

This nigga fucked me straight the fuck out.

Turning slightly, I let the warm jets pulse against my aching pussy. My alarm went off — three hours until departure.

There was a knock at the door.

"Come in," I said.

He opened the door and stepped inside, dick dangling.

"Good morning," he said, walking toward me.

I sat up as he approached. He eased into the tub one foot at a time and sat on the edge, his dick resting limp between his thighs. Thinking about the few hours I had left, I figured I couldn't let all that dick go to waste.

I reached through the water and began stroking him with my towel. His dick pulsed, slowly rising to a full erection. I leaned forward, licking the head, then kissing it. Gripping his waist, I took him into my mouth.

I watched him close his eyes and tilt his head back, savoring the moment. I must've been doing something right because he grabbed my head and started pumping into my mouth. I adjusted my pace—slow, then fast—sucking and smacking until he warned me he was about to cum.

Ready to put on my big-girl panties, I didn't let up. Not one bit. I was in control. I kept him in my mouth as he tried to pull away. While sucking, I jacked him off, knowing exactly what he needed.

He came.

I blew bubbles into the water like I was showing off a trophy.

My dare was complete.

Satisfied, he slid into the tub with me, and we soaked together. I was grateful the tub was big enough for both of us. The suite was comfortable—almost romantic.

When I stepped out, I grabbed another towel and washed my face. While brushing my teeth, I caught his reflection watching me in the mirror. I wondered what was on his mind.

Finished, I left the bathroom and started getting dressed.

Sitting on the bed, brushing my hair, I reflected on the night. Lost in thought, I didn't notice him approach until he sat beside me, startling me just slightly.

He thanked me for an incredible night. I told him the pleasure was all mine. I grabbed his phone, snapped a selfie, and entered my number.

I dressed while he watched. Afterward, I double-checked the room to make sure I hadn't left anything behind. He got dressed, kissed me, and gathered my suitcases, setting them by the door as I called the front desk for BagVIP.

We headed downstairs to check out. The lobby buzzed with people coming and going. That's when I spotted Danielle and Sam waiting.

When they saw us, they smiled and waved.

"Dana, we gotta go—the hotel already handled the bags," Sam said.

"Ladies," I said, "this is a good friend of mine. Antwon, these are my girls—Sam and Danielle."

"Nice to make your acquaintance," he said, kissing their hands.

"So… how was your stay in Vegas?" Sam asked, raising an eyebrow.

"Spectacular," he said, laughing.

"I see," Danielle said. "Someone missed breakfast."

The concierge let us know our cab was ready. We stepped outside, saying goodbye to Sin City. I asked Sam to take a picture of Antwon and me. He pulled me close and kissed me long and deep.

"Don't forget to call," I said as I climbed into the cab.

"I won't," he replied, waving as the cab pulled away.

I watched him fade into the distance, feeling something I hadn't expected as the hotel disappeared behind us.

During the cab ride, I was interrogated—nothing too detailed, just enough to earn all the oohs and aahs. I stared out the window quietly, replaying my night with Antwon.

When we reached the airport, we hugged and cried, promising—as we always did—to keep in touch. Then we departed, once again.

Without a word, two weeks passed. I guess what happens in Vegas stays… in Vegas.

Damn, I wish I had gotten his number. What was I thinking?

Of all my dares, this one backfired. I fell for a man who was charming, intelligent, had a big dick, gave good head, and was a damn good lover. As I flipped through my phone, I reminisced about that night and the day we left. The selfies made it worse—thinking I might never see him again. And the picture of his dick? Pure torture.

That dick was talking to me.

I zoned out, imagining what it would feel like to have him in me just one more time. I'd ride it—like a mechanical bull. I started to delete the pictures, but stopped. That night was one to remember.

The one that got away.

Several years had passed and Danielle's daughter was turning five. It had been a little over a year since Vegas, though it felt longer. I packed my bags and booked my flight. This would be the first time we'd all been together since that trip.

I arrived at the airport three hours early—TSA wasn't about to mess this up. Sitting at the gate, I pulled out my Nook. I was glad I brought it; waiting with nothing to do is the worst.

I was deep into my reading when I noticed the seat next to me was suddenly occupied.

I looked up.

Antwon.

He caught me completely off guard, a lump forming in my throat.

"Well… hello," I said.

Flashbacks hit instantly, but I snapped out of it just as fast—remembering he never called. I tried to ignore him, but his small talk kept breaking my concentration. Finally, I closed my case and turned toward him.

Damn. He was still fine.

"I'm curious," I snapped, unable to help myself. "Why didn't you call?"

Who was I kidding? Our encounter was supposed to be a dare. Yet here I was, feeling salty—as if I'd been played. The hunter caught by the game. My dare was to find him, seduce him, and fuck him.

And somehow, I lost.

He didn't know any of that. So yeah—I was allowed to be mad.

"First," he said calmly, "how have you been?"

"Fine. And you?" I replied, sarcasm heavy.

"You've been on my mind since Vegas," he said. "I really wish I'd met you the first night you arrived. We could've had more time."

That night came rushing back—his tongue, our bodies tangled, fucking until dawn. The memory alone made me shift in my seat.

"You had the opportunity to call," I said, finally looking him dead in the eye.

"Why didn't you?"

"No, wait—let me explain," he said. "My phone got wet and shorted out. I even tried putting it in a bag of rice to dry it out, but that didn't work. I had to buy a new phone, and the backup didn't capture anything. I lost all my pictures, all my contacts—everything. Including you."

He chuckled softly. "Seriously, I've thought about that night. How I got picked up at the bar."

"Picked up?" I said. "What do you mean, *picked up*?"

"Yeah—you picked me up," he said, smiling. "And I'm cool with that. I'm glad you did. I wasn't just turned on by your beauty, but by your mind. When you pulled off in that cab, I wanted to stop you—but I didn't think I had the right."

Then he added, "Oh, and you can believe it or not, I changed my thinking about that little issue we talked about—my father's wishes. I decided to go for my law degree. That was because of you."

"Really," I said dryly. "You don't say."

"When I passed the Bar, I thought about you," he continued. "Being an attorney hasn't been so bad."

"Is that right," I replied.

"So… where are you headed?" he asked.

"I'm going to Columbus for a birthday party. You?" I said.

"With you—if that's okay," he smiled.

"So you just *happen* to have a ticket going where I'm going?" I said. "Don't embarrass me trying to pull some slick shit."

He pulled out his boarding pass. "Gate 304B."

I stared at it, then at him. "How did you find me? This can't be a coincidence."

He nodded. "It took some thinking. I contacted your friend Danielle. We talked."

"Hello, may I speak to Danielle?" I asked.

"This is she," she replied. "Who's speaking?"

"I wasn't sure if she remembered me," he continued, "so I gave her my name. I explained that I met her with you in Vegas. She asked how I got her number and how she could help. She was polite—but wary."

"I apologized for reaching out like that," he said. "I told her I'd been thinking about you for a long time. I mentioned that the night we met, you gave me solid advice—advice that helped me make some major decisions."

He laughed lightly. "Your girl is a tough cookie. Straight-faced. Straight-laced. No jokes. She asked again, *"So how exactly can I help you?"*"

"I told her I lost your number when my phone was destroyed. I even said I searched Facebook and Instagram—nothing. She wasn't buying that either. Gave me the third degree. Then she had the nerve to ask, *"Why now?"*"

"I didn't want to lose my shot," he said, "so I kept explaining. I told her life got busy, things were happening fast. But once things settled, I remembered something."

He paused.

"I found a luggage tag on the ground—the one with her information—after your cab pulled off. I kept it. That's how I reached her."

He looked at me. "So… here we are. And yeah, I apologized if I overstepped, but I've been wanting to reconnect with you for a long time."

There was a long pause before she spoke again. I assumed she was contemplating whether or not to give me your whereabouts. Eventually, she mentioned that y'all would be meeting up in Columbus for a birthday party in a couple of days.

The more I talked—and the more I probably sounded desperate, though she didn't say it—I could tell she was weighing whether or not you'd mind her sharing your information. Apparently, she decided you wouldn't, especially since you'd spoken about me on several occasions.

So she gave me your travel itinerary for that morning: Atlanta Hartsfield Airport, Continental Airlines, Gate 304B, departing at 10:30 a.m. with a layover in Chicago. Before hanging up, she added, *'If you're serious, I suggest you get a move on it,'* and then clicked off the phone.

Can you believe her? She's something else."

"I jumped straight on the internet to track your flight path. And wouldn't you know it—the connecting flight I needed to catch you in Atlanta was booked solid. So, being a little thirsty, I found another airline that could get me here to O'Hare just in time for boarding."

I smiled, shaking my head. "When I woke up this morning, I knew it was going to be a good day because I was finally going to see my girls. What I didn't expect was that it would turn out to be *extra* special—because I'd see you too. What a surprise. I'm glad you made it."

I stood to embrace him just as the pre-boarding announcement echoed through the terminal.

"Good afternoon, passengers. This is the pre-boarding announcement for Flight 1435 to Columbus. We are now inviting passengers traveling with small children and those requiring special assistance to begin boarding at this time. Please have your boarding pass and identification ready. General boarding will begin in approximately ten minutes. Thank you."

I looked up at him. "You ready?"

"Of course I'm ready," he replied. "I lost you once—I dare not lose you again."

Chapter Five

Mr. Telephone Man

There was an eerie feeling in the air, but I couldn't quite put my finger on it. The sky darkened before the clouds opened up with a theatrical display of lightning and rumbling thunder. It rained for at least an hour straight, debris swirling from one end of the street to the next. I stood in my patio doorway, watching the last of the downpour.

After the storm passed, light rain continued to cascade from the heavens, as if someone had turned on a sprinkler system. It was the calm after the storm.

My thoughts drifted back to my Nana and her storytelling, especially her theories about where rain came from. Most of her stories were interesting, but Nana herself was something else. When I was younger, I thought her stories were hilarious. Now, as an adult, looking back, I realize she was dead serious—and maybe even onto something.

She used to connect rain, Mother Nature, and women's moods like they were all cut from the same cloth. Sometimes she couldn't believe the things coming out of her own mouth and would laugh at herself mid-story. Her tales often compare a woman's nature to that of Mother Nature.

One time she said women controlled the world and men were just along for the ride. Another time she said, *"When Mother Nature gets in one of her moods, she withholds rain from the earth—just like women withhold pussy when they're upset or heartbroken."*

Nana was something else.

As far as she was concerned, the power of the pussy was queen—running shit with a force so strong its wrath should never be underestimated.

One thing about her Mother Nature stories was how closely they aligned with a woman's emotional state. But she always reminded me that not all tears were sad tears—sometimes they were tears of joy. Rain cleanses the earth. It helps things grow. That was the nurturer in her.

When I was old enough, she added another layer to the story. She said rain was like a mating call, especially when it splashed against tin roofs across the South. *"Boy, did that spike up the birth rates,"* she'd say, chuckling.

Today, her presence was felt.

Lights out. Telephone lines affected. Internet down. Pure chaos.

She could shut things down—or catapult them into motion.

Based on that downpour, she demanded attention. She was either upset, heartbroken, displeased… or ecstatic. From the sound of it, I was betting heartbreak. It had been a while since we'd seen rain like that.

As her tears pounded the ground, the mist and breeze felt amazing. When the rain stopped, the air grew still and calm. My thermostat shifted from breezy to hot, then from hot to muggy almost instantly. A rainbow appeared as sunlight pierced through the clouds. Suddenly, the power was restored.

That part was good.

The bad part? My internet was still acting up—right as I was about to purchase a fierce pair of Christian Louboutin pumps.

Can't stop Mother Nature.

I had been looking forward to stepping out sharp in my new designer shoes, but if that was going to happen, I needed to contact customer service. Thankfully, the storm spared the cell towers. Had those gone down, things would've been ugly.

Twenty people in the queue, four bars on my phone, I was safe. I still had a line to the outside world. Thank God. If I had waited any longer, my phone would've died. Okay, I'm exaggerating… but it felt like forever.

While on hold, I listened to Beethoven's Fifth Symphony, Mozart's Symphony No. 9, and—

Chopin's… shit, I can't remember the name.
I probably fell asleep during that class. I guess I was a little anxious to get that order in. I could already see myself in them—stompin'.

The representative was courteous, professional even. My appointment was set for tomorrow at 8:15 a.m. Just like that, my entire mood shifted.

There's still hope.

The doorbell rang. Lo and behold, punctual is as punctual does—my savior was right on time.

"Hello, I have an order here regarding problems you're experiencing with your line. I'm going to need access to your pole," he said.

As I opened the door, he stood tall and defined. After showing his credentials, we briefly discussed the service order.

"The gate is to the left," I said, pointing toward the rear of the house.

"Thank you. I'll return shortly," he replied.

Hell, he was talking about climbing a pole. Shit, I need to be climbing his pole. As he walked toward the back, I couldn't help but check out his fine ass.

I had to get a better view.

I closed the door, hurried to the patio, and watched him as he strapped in and climbed the telephone pole. Grabbing my cup of tea, I sat there looking out the window, straight-up stalking him while he worked. He scaled the pole like Spider-Man. His leg muscles were well-developed, I mean tight.

The hard hat and tool belt pulled my focus next, reminding me of a Village Person. Shit, my thirsty ass—there wasn't even a Telephone Man in the Village People. But I guess the hard hat and tool belt did it for me. That body, that swag—pure masculinity in every sense.

The phone rang, startling me. I was so engrossed in watching *my* Telephone Man that I let it ring. If it was important, they'd call back. Besides, it would probably go to voicemail.

Then I saw him hold up his handset, signaling it was him calling.

Oh shit… yeah, that's him.

The phone rang again. Embarrassing. I wondered if he knew I was watching.

Duh.

"Hello," I answered, trying to play it cool.

"I fixed the problem," he said. "It was on the outside. I just wanted to make sure there were no issues with your phone set. Everything seems to be working properly. I'll be in—give me a minute."

Damn. He sounded just as good on the phone as he looked in person.

After hanging up, I went back to the patio and watched him until he approached the porch door. I invited him in and offered him something to drink. The humidity was heavy after the rain—I would've thought it'd cool down by now. He was soaked.

"I'll take some ice water, if you don't mind," he said. "It's gotten pretty warm out there. May I sit here for a minute?"

He sat down and began filling out his report and invoice.

I took a seat at the kitchen island across from him while he completed the paperwork. When he handed me the invoice, I reached forward and accidentally knocked over his glass of ice water.

"Is everything okay?" he asked.

"Yes sorry about that. Let me clean this up. I'll get you another glass."

Shit, better now than never, I thought.

"I'm sure you receive compliments all the time—advances from others. I just want to say… I find you very attractive."

He looked stunned by my forwardness.

"Yeah, I've gotten a few compliments here and there, but never this directly, not from a customer," he replied.

"My mother always said a *closed mouth doesn't get fed*," I said. "I hope you don't mind."

The only thing stopping this union was our clothes, so they needed to be removed from the equation.

I stepped directly in front of him and unraveled the belt of my dress. As it slid from my shoulders, the fabric floated to the floor and pooled at my feet. I moved closer—close enough for him to push his chair back from the table. The moment he did, I straddled him.

Staring in disbelief, his pants began to betray him. I leaned in, kissed his ear, and whispered, "Give it here—and don't say nothin'."

He reached up, cupping my breast as I unzipped his pants. Sensing his urgency, I lifted slightly to give him room to maneuver. He tugged his khakis down to his knees, revealing just how excited he was. The hard-on pressing against his boxers made that obvious.

I reached past him to the utility drawer and grabbed a condom.

Yeah, some people might wonder who keeps condoms in the kitchen. I do.
They're stored in every room of my house. You never know when—or where—the mood will strike. Like right now.

In one smooth motion, I tore open the wrapper and held the condom between my teeth. Dropping to my knees, I rolled it carefully over the head and down his shaft, controlling his movements so he didn't push too far and make me gag.

I climbed back onto his lap as he sat, guiding himself in until he was fully engulfed. As we locked together, I felt the full force of him hitting all the right spots while I rocked back and forth. No stranger to the rodeo, I lifted and slowed until I found my rhythm.

His hands gripped my hips as we synchronized into a steady rocking motion.

He played volley with my breasts, sucking my nipples and sending shockwaves through my body. With my feet planted firmly on the floor, I used his thighs as leverage, rising and falling in search of that perfect ten.

There were moments when the urge to cum surged hard, but I wasn't ready to end this yet. Controlling the climax felt like resisting an itch that demanded attention. Once that build-up hits a certain point, there's no turning back—and I wanted more.

There was something deeply satisfying about exercising my sexual prowess. I loved the dick, yes—but mastering the positions, controlling the pace, claiming the moment—that fed me in another way.

I turned, presenting my back to him, still gyrating as he remained hard. He cupped my pussy and rubbed my clit, intensifying the pleasure. I placed my hand over his as we stroked together. He kissed my back, dragging his tongue slowly up my spine.

As I neared the edge, he whispered, "Not yet."

We moved to the chaise in the living room. Dropping to his knees, he began to suck and lick me. Each pass of his tongue weakened my legs, every touch making me more sensitive than the last. My body started to spasm as I squirmed, holding his head firmly between my thighs.

The feeling was too good to release.

"You like this pussy?" I asked.

"Yeah," he murmured. "I like it a lot. It's like sucking nectar flowing straight from the heavens."

"Go round and round with your tongue," I moaned. "Oh… ahhh… right there. Don't stop."

I tried to delay my climax for as long as possible, but realistically, I couldn't hold back any longer. His head was the best thing I'd had in a long time. In moments like this, that adage rang true: *free the mind and your ass will follow*. I let go of every inhibition.

The nastier I talked to him, the more aroused I became. I gyrated faster and harder as he sealed his lips around my clit. Adrenaline surged through me, my pussy throbbing as the orgasm built steadily. I felt the twitching intensify, each pulse stronger than the last, until my muscles contracted in rhythmic waves.

Then it hit.

My body stiffened as I was thrown into a full orgasm. After I reached my peak, the intensity slowly eased, tapering off until it finally stopped. My entire body went limp. I was drenched, my heart still racing before it gradually began to settle.

When he touched my arm, my trance shattered and the fantasy evaporated. His lips moved, but whatever he said barely registered.

"Are you all, right?" he asked.

I shook my head slightly. "Yeah… sorry. What did you say?"

"By signing here, you're indicating that you're satisfied with the repairs today and that your services have been restored," he said, handing me the work order.

As I signed the form, the scent of his cologne lingered in the air. There's just something about a man's cologne that does it for me.

His visit was short—but sweet.

I shook his hand and walked him to the door. Before leaving, he handed me his business card and told me to call the company if I had any other issues or needed further assistance.

I experienced many sleepless nights after he departed. I tossed and turned, stuck in a constant state of limbo. With my hands clutched between my thighs, masturbating took the edge off—but it wasn't the same as having the real deal: a man's tongue or his dick.

Imagining him in my mind's eye—entering my room, standing naked with a full erection—was the perfect way to relieve some of my sexual tension. Having a vivid imagination helped to a certain degree, but there was still something missing.

My bullet.

I reached over to the nightstand, retrieved it, and powered it at a low speed so I could build gradually toward my climax. The multiple speeds were everything. Between the bullet and my imagination, I figured I could manage for the time being.

The mind is a powerful thing.

I spread my legs and placed the bullet on my clit. The vibrations sent waves of sensation throughout my body. As I worked it against my clit, I felt it swell and harden. I slid my fingers into my pussy, stroking myself, sometimes pumping, sometimes teasing.

My mind went blank imagining nothing but him, replaying sexual acts that took me to another level. With him fixed in my thoughts, I began gyrating my hips, intensifying the stimulation as I increased the speed another notch.

My focus shifted inward. I talked myself through the sensation, begging for my release as I cried out, "Ohhh… cum… fuck that pussy."

But my fingers weren't enough. I needed something thicker.

I reached for Chocolate Thunder to join the session. Thunder lived up to his name—rich, dark, 9¾ inches, thick, with a realistic head and veins. Using my vaginal muscles, I pushed him out and pulled him back in, rotating Thunder in slow circles.

When he hit *that* spot, my clit twitched violently as my vaginal muscles began contracting hard. My body convulsed as I came—deep, powerful, and uncontrollable. The pleasure overwhelmed me, and I rolled onto my side, curling into a fetal position as my pussy tightened around Thunder.

As the climax faded, so did his image.

The quieter my fantasy became, the louder my heartbeat sounded in my ears. I tried to summon his image again, but after such an intense release, it wouldn't return. I knew it would take time before I could reach that place again.

Damn.

I had just served myself hot sex on a platter, and for the moment, I was good.

Lying there, I couldn't help but wonder how different it would have been if he were there with me.

After work, I stopped by Giant Eagle to pick up a few items for dinner. I was mentally checking off my list when I thought I saw *him* pass by. Were my eyes playing tricks on me? I could've sworn I saw him heading down the cereal aisle.

Or maybe I was just thirsty and imagining things.

He wasn't there.

I slowed my pace, just in case I ran into him. The last thing I wanted was for him to think I was stalking.

Instead—who should appear but Mrs. Washington. Lord, that woman could *talk*. And when I say talk, I mean she could *go*. I tried to avoid a long, drawn-out conversation, but of course she struck one up anyway. She noticed my Red Bottoms and immediately launched a whole commentary about my shoes.

Total cock block.

From there, she went on about the weather, the people down the street—just anything. I didn't want to be rude, but I had to cut her short. She clearly had trouble taking hints, so I had to be direct.

"Well, Mrs. Washington, it was good seeing you, but I've got to run. Take care," I said, already moving down the aisle.

If it *was* him, he was probably long gone by now.

Damn.

Oh well. Let me hurry up and find this rice so I can get my ass out of here.

"Miss, where can I find boil-in-the-bag rice?" I asked an employee.

"About the middle of aisle eleven."

I headed down aisle eleven and bent down to grab a box of rice when I heard a familiar voice.

"Ms. Dawson, how are you?"

I looked over my shoulder—and there he was.

"Mr. Whitfield," I said with a nod. "How are you?"

"I'm doing great. And you?" he replied. "Have you had any more trouble with your phone line?"

"No, thanks to you," I said.

"Remember, if you have any more problems, just give me a call," he added. "You do still have my card, right?"

"Yes, I'll keep that in mind."

He smiled. "You don't have to be so formal. Please—call me Arlon. I'm not at work right now. We can move beyond formalities, don't you think?"

"All right, Arlon," I said. "I'd like that. And call me Cherrie."

I reached into my purse and pulled out a business card. "Here—take my number."

He glanced at it. "So you're a personal shopper, huh?"

"Yes," I said. "I do specialty retail services. I shop for clients who don't have the time—home décor, fashion, things like that. A lot of times, I also act as a consultant, providing direct services. If you ever need anything, feel free to give me a call."

While I was explaining what I did for a living, he looked at me with a glazed expression on his face, as if he were looking right through me. Strangely enough, it felt kind of nice. He seemed vulnerable.

"Thanks, I'll keep you in mind," he said, slipping my business card into his wallet. "Well, I see you're busy right now, so I won't keep you. It was nice seeing you again. Uh… maybe I'll give you a call later."

"All right, do that—and have a good day," I replied.

As he walked away, I found myself thinking, *maybe?* What does *maybe* mean? Either you're going to call, or you're not. Still, I hoped he would. I guess I'll just wait and see what happens.

Besides, I still have his number.

I lay there thinking about Arlon and our brief encounter at the store. It was short but sweet. Who would have thought I'd run into him at the grocery store—what luck! Oh my God, he was wearing *those* shorts. Ooo wee… and those arms. That man knows he has a body. Damn, he looked good.

I began to drift off while listening to 93.1 WZAK, *For Lovers Only.* Funny enough, I dreamed the other night that the two of us were standing at the bedroom door, trying to decide who should enter first. Rock, paper, scissors—I won. I walked into the room, slowly undressed, and lay down on the bed in a state of anticipated passion.

Unlike past dreams, we actually made love. It wasn't just a good fuck—this orgasm was different. It was intense, deeper… more like love and spiritual transcendence. A full-body orgasm. With me on top, the thrill of us engaging in lovemaking sent waves throughout my body. It went beyond the flesh—this was something else entirely. The kind that creeps up on you unexpectedly, like an aftershock.

I woke up in a sweat, heart racing, breathing heavy—like I'd really made love. *Wow... what a dream.* Better yet—*what an orgasm?* I thought, rolling over, trying to fall back asleep. I was floating.

Just as I tried to hold on to that feeling, the phone rang.

"Damn!" I muttered, reaching for my cell. I glanced at the clock—one o'clock in the morning. *Who the fuck is calling me at this hour?*

"Hello," I said groggily.

"I'm sorry if I'm disturbing you. I know it's late, but I had to call," Arlon said.

"No, I wasn't asleep," I lied smoothly, even though I knew it was him. "Who is this?"

"Arlon."

"Arlon... it's one o'clock. Is everything all right?" I asked.

"First, I want to say it was nice seeing you again."

"Likewise. The pleasure was mine."

"There was something I wanted to say when you opened the door the other day," he continued. "But I had to remain professional. It's not often I come across someone as impressive as you. And then seeing you at the store... I wanted to say something then too, but I didn't have the nerve. I didn't want to come off too forward."

"Really?" I said.

"Please let me finish before I change my mind," he sighed heavily. "Here it is—I've thought about you every day since our first encounter. More than once, I wanted to come by your house, but I knew that wouldn't be appropriate. I had your number on the work order and almost called, but that didn't feel right either. So instead, I laid in bed torturing myself… imagining what it would be like to really get to know you."

"Wow… I'm flattered," I said. "Honestly, I've been thinking about you too. Maybe we could get together sometime…?"

"Can I come over?" he asked.

That was fast, I thought. I wasn't expecting that so soon. *Look who's talking,* Ms. *A Closed Mouth Doesn't Get Fed.*

"When would you like to come over?" I asked.

"Well, I have the rest of the weekend off," Arlon said. "If it's not asking too much… how about now?"

I paused for half a second, just long enough to pretend I was considering it.

"Okay," I said. "That's fine with me. I'll see you in a few."

"I'll be there in a minute," he replied.

I jumped out of bed and rushed into the bathroom to freshen up. As the water hit my skin, I laughed to myself.

Patience is a virtue… but apparently, not tonight.

After last night's hookup, I figured it was only fitting that I cooked breakfast. Breakfast is the food of champions. I laid everything out—scrambled cheese eggs, toast, beef sausage, and grits. I stood at the stove wearing his shirt, which barely covered my ass.

He entered the kitchen before I had a chance to fix his plate. Coming up behind me, he wrapped his strong arms around my waist, pulling me into him and kissing my neck. A girl could get used to this, I thought.

"Here, let me fix your plate," he said. "After a morning like this, a King is entitled to serve his Queen. I insist. Besides, we have the rest of the weekend. I'm going to show you how it's done. I got this—so sit back and relax."

He moved effortlessly around the kitchen, fixing our plates while I sat there, savoring the moment.

Somebody pinch me and wake the fuck up, I thought.

This time, I wasn't dreaming.

Nana always said there would be days like this.

After reading Maya's letter, my dick was hard. Jacking off while staring at her picture, I imagined her legs gapped, pussy wet, my dick buried deep inside her. Damn, I missed the fuck out of her. I couldn't wait to get home and fuck her again.

Once I busted my nut, I took a long whiff of her perfume before folding the letter back up. I kissed her picture, then closed my eyes.

Morning came fast. I ate, handled my business, and headed back to my cell. I pulled the rest of her letters from my pocket and started reading. The Jones was back—and this time it was worse. Her words stayed with me, crawling under my skin. My dick stayed hard, and I was constantly adjusting myself just from thinking about her.

Walking around with that kind of tension wasn't smart either. I didn't want anybody getting the wrong impression—or me having to whip somebody's ass over it. Truth was, not getting no pussy made me mean. Sometimes jacking off was the only thing keeping me balanced.

If I wasn't in the shower and didn't have lotion or Vaseline, I had to improvise. When I was sent to the hole, there was nothing. No lube, no comfort—just Maya's pictures and my imagination. I did what I had to do. Palmalina and her five friends—fuck four, I needed all the help I could get.

Pre-cum only worked for so long. Soap did the trick, but the dryness made shit rough. Still, I made it work.

I needed to get the fuck out of here and get some real pussy. Just looking at her picture made me hard, especially when I was alone. I thought about the first time we fucked. I was tired as hell and hadn't had pussy in forever—but none of that mattered. Pressure will bust a pipe.

For two days straight, I jacked my dick raw. Sex is physical and psychological—you need both. One without the other ain't enough. Stud slid me some hooch, which didn't help the situation. Shit just made it worse. Every thought of her naked, her thick ass riding me, had me heated all over again.

I couldn't remember what day it was—just that I'd been here long enough to count meals instead of time. My mind was starving for conversation. My body was starving for her touch.

No matter how hard I got looking at her pictures, I couldn't keep jacking off. It felt like I was rubbing my skin off. Spit and everything else stopped working. Push-ups and sit-ups became my escape—kept my body tight and my mind off fucking.

Dinner came, and I wasn't hungry. I was horny. But discipline mattered, so I ate anyway. When I glanced at the dessert section, the creaminess of the applesauce set my mind wandering. I took some back with me.

Later that night, I pulled out her picture again.

I made do with what I had.

Trevor's boys tried to corner the cigarette market. Some niggas never learn. Just because that motherfucker tried me—and tried to fuck with my brother—I had to make him understand he wasn't that man.

The next morning after count, I checked on Dice. He was straight. Nobody had stepped to him. Later, out in the yard, I sat where I usually did with my people when he asked to talk. Once I agreed, my boys peeled off and gave us space.

We talked for a long time and finally buried the hatchet.

He told me the real reason he carried so much hate toward me. That shit came from bitterness—his mother abandoning him. He admitted he was jealous, envious, angry over what he thought I had and he didn't. Truth was, if his dumb ass hadn't been so focused on sabotaging everything, he would've seen we were in the same boat. He had what I had all along.

I told him he didn't need to feel that way. Moms loved both of us and raised him like her own. He admitted that his anger had blinded him—kept him from seeing what was right in front of his face. I told him if anyone had the right to be pissed, it should've been me. Then again, I had my own anger issues.

His moms knew our father was married. She knew what she was doing when she broke up my home.

We hugged it out, letting go of all the bullshit that had haunted us our whole lives. That moment sealed the truce. Funny how a crisis can do that—bring clarity. All those years of tension and resentment, we could've been building something instead of tearing each other down.

With that settled, it was time to knock Trevor off his ivory tower.

That night, laying in my bunk staring at the ceiling, my mind started working overtime. What sells inside and outside the commissary that nobody had locked down?

Sex.

Niggas in here starving. I knew how I was when I was boxed in—tight, restless, angry. Dudes out here losing their minds because they ain't touched a woman in years. Some don't get mail at all. Others get hit with Dear John letters and release papers in the same envelope.

Maya's letters kept me sane.

If I could build something around that need… I could shift the whole balance.

I wrote Maya and asked if she could round up a few of her girls—take some pictures, write erotic *To Whom It May Concern* letters. Then I thought about the dudes who lean the other way. A lot of niggas in here grew up behind bars and don't know nothing else.

Capitalism don't stop at the gate. Supply and demand is everywhere.

Maya's cousin Pookie was perfect. He wouldn't mind writing letters and posing for a few shots—especially if there was money in it. No conjugal visits in this bitch. It had been years since some of these dudes saw anything close to intimacy.

Note to self: separate envelopes.

I had the inside hook to get everything past administration. No mistakes. No sloppiness. I was about to own this market.

Two weeks later, mail call was beautiful.

Along with Maya's regular letters, I had envelopes—ten female, six male. Prices varied depending on content, pictures, and whether someone wanted a pen pal. Within a month, I was killing it. I even got the library hookup to make copies.

Some dudes didn't care if the letters were identical, they just wanted mail.

Dice looked at me sideways. I thought we were past that. Still, I shared the wealth. Made sure he had cigarettes, snacks, and money on his books until release. I didn't owe him that—but he was my brother, and I wasn't about to let envy turn into distraction.

Trevor still had his cigarette hustle, but I was out-earning him. Niggas would borrow a smoke just to look at some pictures before spending their last cigarette.

Release day was coming. Two nights and a wake-up.

I sat my cellie down and told him how much I appreciated him—how he always had my back. I passed the operation to him and told him how to reach me if he needed more. Loyalty deserves loyalty.

Trevor walked around mean-mugging like his whole world had tilted.

That shit was hilarious.

Spud went home first. Then Stud. Then Dice.

I was the last one left from the original crew.

Life is funny like that the lessons you learn in crisis. I learned a lot in that place.

Even though I damn sure wasn't guilty.

As I walked out those doors, I wasn't the same angry man who walked in. I gained a lot of wisdom inside those walls. The first thing I saw when I entered was a phrase painted above the door:

"Gold is tried by fire, brave men by adversity."

Back then, it sounded like mumbo jumbo. Standing there now, ready to leave, that shit was crystal clear.

I was going home stronger. Wiser.

Despite the interruption to my life, I did accomplish something. I built a mini-empire—thanks to Maya. I met some solid brothers. I buried the hatchet with Dice. And I missed my moms, my pops, and my woman more than anything.

When the doors opened, the first face I saw in that lobby was Maya's. She stood there with her arms open, ready to receive me on my first day of freedom. The moment she touched me, I melted. I bent down and kissed her, feeling a rush I hadn't known in a long time.

As we walked to the car, she handed me the keys. I drove away and didn't look back—just closed another chapter of my life.

Once home, I went straight to the bedroom, stripped down, and stretched across the bed while Maya ran my bath. I couldn't wait to soak in privacy. She had the house lit just right, burning one of my favorite fragrance tarts—Taylor Made's Pi Type by Givenchy. I eased into the tub, bubbles swallowing me whole, washing away the stench of incarceration.

The jets pulsed against my body as I relaxed. Damn, I missed this kind of peace. I had my freedom—and my woman.

The water shifted as Maya sat on the edge of the tub, legs parted, waiting. Feeling myself get hard, I sat up. This was the moment I'd been holding onto. I leaned forward, diving in, letting instinct take over. She wanted it just as bad as I did.

Fully aroused, I stepped out of the tub, grabbed her hand, and pulled her toward the bedroom, both of us eager. I laid her at the edge of the bed, pulled her closer, and worked slowly and deliberately. Watching her squirm fed something deep inside me. I took my time, savoring the way she moved beneath me, the way she responded.

Tears streamed down Maya's face as I rubbed myself against her, raw emotion pouring out of her. That vulnerability touched me. I'd waited too long for this moment to rush it.

I closed my eyes and guided myself in, grounding my breath. There was a lot running through my head. She looked fragile, and the hunger I felt had to be balanced with care. I reminded myself to slow down, to be present.

Inside those walls, I'd turned into something else—hard, ruthless, built to survive. Two lungs and no heart. I had to be.

But standing here now, free, with Maya beneath me, I found my heart again.

Getting mine mattered. But making sure she felt everything at first mattered more.

I moved steadily, controlled, letting the rhythm build naturally. We moved together, long and deep, connected in a way that went beyond the physical. When she finally let go, her body shaking as she reached her peak, it pulled me right with her.

Everything hit at once.

I came hard, a full-body release, shockwaves rolling from head to toe. I collapsed into the moment, breathless, grounded, whole.

Damn.

Just like I knew it would be.

Cuddling with Maya was priceless. Shit, she had me calling her name. Lying there, replaying my day, I realized how grateful I was to have a woman I could depend on. Maya was special—special in a way that mattered. I think I loved her. Making love to her grounded me, centered me. I hated that we couldn't spend the rest of the day wrapped up in bed, but I knew Moms and Pops had something planned, and we needed to be there.

We cleaned up and headed to my parents' house for my welcome-home cookout. Everybody showed up. My niggas—Spud, Stud, and Slice—came through with their girls. The rest of the set was posted up out front. Dice was there too, with Maya's girl Nicole, the one who'd been writing to him while we were locked down. When I walked in, he stood up and greeted me like a brother should. Moms and Pops exchanged a look and smiled.

The smell of barbecue filled the air. I couldn't wait to get a plate—my mom's mac and cheese and my pops' beef Western ribs. Pops cooked them so tenderly the meat fell right off the bone.

Dice pulled me to the side and thanked me for having his back inside. It took prison for him to realize we needed each other as brothers, especially when shit hit the fan. Fuck the bullshit. He thought I was just going to let Trevor and his punk ass crew dog him out. A motherfucker would've died that day. He wasn't about to be anybody's bitch—and neither was I.

When I hugged him, my eyes burned. After all those years growing up under the same roof, raised by the same parents, living with bitterness, we finally found our way back to each other.

I am my brother's keeper.

Later, I went down to the prosecutor's office to straighten out the discrepancy. I waited over an hour before they finally called my name. The prosecutor stepped out, calling for me. I stood and walked toward him, hand extended.

He stopped short.

"Who are you?" he asked.

"You called Andre Johnson," I said.

"Yes, but you're not the Andre Johnson in my file," he said, checking again.

At the time of my arrest, I was wearing a beard. My brother and I look so much alike, people have mistaken us for twins. Thinking back, I could see how an eyewitness might've made that mistake—but it still didn't sit right with me. My brother had the warrant. A witness picked *me* out of a lineup on some humble shit. I'd been telling them from day one.

Pulling out my release paperwork, I said, "I was instructed to meet with you today at 2 p.m. after leaving the facility."

He frowned. "I've never seen you before. There must be an error. I was out on personal leave. The case was reassigned."

These motherfuckers should've caught that shit a long time ago. My court-appointed attorney had rolled over and died on me. "That's what I told them when they arrested me," I snapped. "I did time because nobody wanted to listen."

"Come with me," he said. "Let's get this sorted out."

I followed him into his office and took a seat across from him. He flipped through the file, asked for my date of birth, place of birth, and whether I knew Andrez Johnson.

"That's my brother," I told him.

He sighed, apologized, and admitted someone had made a typo on a warrant. Instead of correcting it, they kept *my* information attached. I spent over a year locked up for something I didn't do.

Walking back to my car, I made a call.

"As-salāmu ʿalaykum wa raḥmatullāhi wa barakātuhu, Abdul.

Yeah—this is Deuce. Welcome back, brother. Listen, I need you. I'm suing the State for wrongful conviction. I need you to represent me."

Chapter Six
My Brother's Keeper

Flossed and polished, we rolled in five rows deep—jackets poppin' green and gold, Deuce Boys fifteen strong in this bitch. Spectators watched as we kicked our stands. Make no mistake about it, we did our thing and were well respected.

The smell of barbecue floated through the air. The sun was shining brightly, and waves from Lake Erie brushed calmly against the break walls. Bikers mingled, drinking, laughing, stunting their colors. The set with the most colors at count won a trophy. Music blasted through the park, EPMD's *You Gots to Chill* pumping heavy.

The annual MC picnic at Gordon Park had a huge turnout. Booty shorts, spandex, and cleavage stretched as far as the eye could see. I rode up solo—but I had no intention of leaving alone.

"Look at that dime over there," I said, pointing north at a thick, short hottie. "I need to flip that coin."

"Yo, Kid, what the fuck that mean?" Slice blurted.

"I need some head and some tail," I joked.

Spud chuckled. "You stoooopid for that one, Kid."

"Nah," Slice smirked. "That nigga corny as fuck."

Across the park stood Dice and his fucked-up crew. That nigga couldn't stand me, and I couldn't stand his ass either. Fuck him—mad because he ain't done shit with his life. But today wasn't that. The bullshit was checked at the gate.

We were all brothers today.

We came to eat, listen to good music, check out new bikes and lids, and see who left with who. Still, I had a fucked-up feeling he'd be on some bitch shit. That was his MO. Everything had to be a competition. He was the type to sneak you if he caught you slipping. I kept one eye open.

"Damn, that's a lot of ass," I said.

"Ten asses to be exact," Spud replied.

"What set reps chocolate and pink?"

"Diamond's Angels," Slice said. "That's what they call themselves."

"How you know?"

"My cousins in that group," he said proudly.

"Look at the ass on the leader," I said. "Goddamn—she thick."

Just then, they stopped in unison, kicked their stands, and dismounted. She removed her helmet, and her hair spilled down her back.

She glowed.

Small frame. Tight waist. Thick hips—perfectly balanced.

"Who is that?" I asked.

"Fuck if I know," Spud said.

"Man, she gorgeous," I said, pointing.

"Y'all bitches sitting here gawking," Spud said. "I'm about to get names. Fuck what you heard."

He walked off.

Slice followed. I stood there a second too long, caught in a trance. Too cool to run, I took my time before catching up. They weren't going anywhere. Things were just getting started.

My mission was names and numbers. I had game—and nobody who knew me knew what it was.

"Hey, Deuce!" someone yelled.

"Give me a minute," I said. "I'll get with you."

She stood next to her bike, eyes scanning the crowd.

Damn, she was fine.

I hadn't seen her before. I checked for a *Property Of* patch—nothing. That was good. She wasn't claimed by anyone in our circle.

Open invitation.

I extended my hand. "Deuce. And you are?"

Maya, she said. "Pleased to meet you."

Beautiful name. Beautiful woman.

"Maya," I said, flashing my million-dollar smile, "that's a perfect name for a woman like you."

She raised an eyebrow. "Is that the best you got? That line really works for you?"

I laughed. "Honestly? I came up with that when you pulled up. It wasn't rehearsed. You inspired it."

"Wow," she said, smirking. "There you go again. Let's start over—minus the corny."

She waved her hand dismissively.

I liked that.

She wasn't easy. Not the type impressed just because I was Deuce. In this circle, my name carried weight—but she didn't know my reputation, and that was fine.

I wanted her to know *me*.

And that was going to take a little more work.

We slipped off to the side and started sharing information. She was from the West Coast and had moved to Cleveland a year ago with her cousin to attend Cleveland State University. She was a sophomore. Some things she didn't even have to say were obvious. She had a beautiful smile, nice white teeth, and when she opened her mouth, her conversation was sharp.

I was impressed.

Better yet—I was intrigued.

She was smart *and* fine as fuck.

I had to let her know I was interested. That was my mission. The Deuce Boys were popular, and plenty of women wanted to get at us—but right now, my eyes were on the prize.

In the days that followed, we had several conversations, filling in the gaps. We went on a few dates, and I stepped my game up, letting her know she should be with me. Our dates were different. We bent corners together, laughed together, and—believe it or not—slept together.

No sex.

We spent quality time. When we laid down, we stayed wrapped in each other's arms, talking for hours until we drifted off to sleep. There was something different about Maya. Most women I fuck on the first night—it's all about the pussy. Don't get me wrong, I love pussy. But with her, I wanted more.

I shared more with her than I ever had with anyone else. Outside of my boys and my family, nobody really knew me. To other women, I was just Deuce—the fine nigga with the fly Harley. My life had always been private, and quiet as kept, I wanted it to stay that way.

What surprised me was how much I genuinely wanted to know her as a person. This wasn't a booty call. It was about learning her mind before touching her body. Don't get it twisted—I knew when the time came, I was going to fuck the shit out of her and satisfy every need she had.

Who was I fooling? I *could* have fucked her on the first night. But she was strong-willed, and it took longer than usual. She told me she didn't want to rush anything, and I respected that. So I didn't push her—even though I wanted her bad.

As a result, many nights I drove straight home and took cold showers, bone motherfuckin' hard.

Patience is a virtue—or so they say. I'd be ready when she was ready.

Being a Deuce Boy came with perks. Pussy was never hard to come by. As my relationship with Maya grew, ex-flings and potentials started feeling some type of way about the time I was spending with her. I made it clear—my interest was in *her*, and nobody else.

More importantly, I tried to show her that it wasn't all about sex, even though I *wanted* to fuck. She understood that.

Truth be told, I was tempted. I'm a man.

Being left with multiple erections could easily push me toward other women. She told me she understood my dilemma and said if I wanted to fuck, I could—that she wouldn't be mad.

Yeah… women say that shit all the time.

When it happens, suddenly you're wrong.

I knew it was a test. And I had chosen her.

Life throws a lot of tests at you, but this one? This motherfuckin' test was a *bitch*.

Still, if waiting was the price, I'd pay it. I decided to abstain.

Hopefully, I don't fail.

In the meantime, I've spent a whole lot of time jacking off. Just know—when the time comes, she better fuck the shit outta me.

We had been dating for a while, and one thing was certain—we had grown closer. It felt like she had opened her heart to me. Anyone who saw us together would've assumed we were a couple with all kissing and touching. One thing I knew for sure—Maya had done wonders for my ego.

Life was good.

She gave me that extra push I needed to move forward. For a long time, I'd been thinking about expanding my business—opening a biker's club. Not some hole-in-the-wall spot, but something real nice. I had looked at properties before but never followed through.

When Maya came into my life, I started seeing things differently.

I bought my first piece of property—the old YMCA on St. Clair. It became the new home of the Deuce Boys MC. Ample parking, a party room, a swimming pool, and office space made it perfect for business.

After grueling hours and intense labor, renovations were finally complete, and the grand opening was approaching.

Everybody showed up for the opening—members with their ladies on their arms, me included. The bar was poppin'. DJ Krunk was on the wheels, cuttin' up. The turnout was solid, and we made good money. By last call, cleanup was underway, doors locked within the hour.

My bed was calling.

As soon as I got home, I didn't even think the door fully closed before I started stripping. Clothes came off everywhere, snatching, dropping, moving fast. I made a beeline for the shower. Maya fussed behind me, picking up my clothes while I focused on one thing—washing the grime off.

Once I hit the shower, it was over.

Muscles tensed, I leaned forward and let the jets pound my back. Warm, pulsating water massaged the tension out of me. Still sexually frustrated, I started stroking my dick.

Maya stood outside the door watching for a moment—then joined me.

I wasn't expecting that.

My heart started racing when I saw her standing naked in the doorway. This waiting shit had been whipping my ass, and jacking off only did so much. Feeling something other than Palmalina and her four friends was more than welcome.

I was exhausted—didn't even know if my dick would respond if I wanted it to. Of all nights, *this* was when she decided to finally give me some pussy, and I was tired as fuck.

But seeing her naked?

My motherfuckin' dick got hard without hesitation.

I checked myself—*tired?* Fool, you better get it while the getting's good. You done waited this long. Fuck being tired.

I invited her in.

Water cascaded down her body, flowing smoothly along her legs. Maya washed my back, then moved to the front—my chest, my stomach, and eventually my dick. I got so hot I snatched the towel from her and tossed it over the rack.

Soap suds covered us as I pulled her close, kissing her deeply. It was time to stop playing games and start fucking.

Even worn out, I rinsed off and gathered enough energy to make it to bed. Lying there, Maya kissed my eyelids, my lips—our tongues tangled passionately. All I could think was how worth it the wait had been.

She kissed my nipples, my stomach, then my belly button. Each slow, sensual kiss sent waves of pleasure through my body.

My dick flinched as I anticipated her luscious lips embracing me. She began caressing my inner thighs, creating a slow, deliberate trail straight to it. Standing erect, she licked around the ridge of my head, then gently licked and sucked my balls. I thought I was going to pass out from the intensity of pleasure. I'd had my dick sucked by many women, but for some reason, I couldn't remember anyone ever licking or sucking my balls like this. Then again, Maya wasn't just any girl. There was tenderness in what she did—care behind every move.

She dragged her tongue from the base of my shaft to the head. When she hit that spot, my arousal surged. I began moving my dick into her mouth, grinding slowly, up and down. As she sucked me, I heard her moan—like she'd found her rhythm. The sound sent chills up my spine.

I lifted her, repositioning her, and she took me all in—deep-throating me while jacking me off until I was right at my peak. When I told her I was about to cum, she stopped and climbed on top of me instead. She rode me until I screamed her name.

Ain't that a bitch!

After busting that nut, all the tension drained from my body. Lying there, replaying the experience, my mind kept going back to how well she gave head. Having my dick in her mouth was satisfying, but somehow, it wasn't enough. My dick pressed against her ass, already ready for another round.

Maya turned over and mounted me again. Her pussy was so juicy it was effortless sliding in and out. I eased into her slowly at first. Her face reflected pure bliss as she worked her muscles—squeezing and releasing while I fucked her.

She was ripe and ready, gliding up and down, lubing me with every stroke. I watched her breasts bounce with each movement. I grabbed her hips, helping her stay in rhythm as she rested her ass against my thighs. She rolled her hips until I felt a deep, warm sensational tingling pressure building fast.

I pushed upward as she leaned back, legs spread in the air, while I worked that pussy. She arched her legs over my thighs as I pounded away. The shit was good—damn good to me. And judging by her moans and the way her body responded, the dick was good to her too.

For a moment, I lost all control, riding it out as my nut exploded inside Maya. Every ounce of energy drained from my body. All I could do was roll over. If she had asked for another round, I would've had to respectfully decline and tap the fuck out.

Every muscle in my body felt spent.

I pulled her close, cuddled up behind her, kissed her softly, and we both drifted into a deep sleep. The sex was excellent—Maya lived up to every expectation I had imagined.

I slept like a baby.

Every month, each MC takes a turn hosting a night at their clubhouse. If you're invited, you're obligated to attend—or your house gets fined. We always showed up for other clubs, and this month, Circle Night landed at the Deuces, aka Da Dub Shack.

One rule everybody respects: it's all about respect—as long as it ain't a rival club, who gives a fuck. This Saturday night was like any other, except we had guests in the house—invitation only.

DJ Corkscrew had the tables blazing. Old-school hip hop filled the room—*Paul Revere, Eric B. for President,* joints like that. Rounds were bought and passed around. The atmosphere was live, people laughing, vibing, enjoying themselves.

I had a few drinks, just enough to be social. I don't like drinking heavily while I'm working. You never know when shit might pop off—

some nigga getting out of line, disrespecting me or my members. I stayed alert, especially knowing who *might* walk through that door: Dice and his boys.

That's always the problem. His ass wasn't invited—and on top of that, he brings his crew like he owns the place. Thinks he got it like that.

Heat crept up my collar.

Standing at the end of the bar, zoning out, something told me this night was headed somewhere bad. I could feel it in my guts.

Maya wrapped her arms around my waist. At 5'5", the warmth of her body instantly cooled my temperature. She didn't even realize how much I needed her right then. Her presence grounded me—kept me balanced. Tonight, I needed that.

Aside from security escorting a group out for smoking weed in the bathroom, things were smooth. You could tell folks were enjoying themselves—empty bottles lining the bar, shot glasses everywhere, chatter bouncing off the walls.

Right before last call, the police showed up.

Of course they did.

They started fucking with people, asking for IDs. Then Alcohol Beverage Control rolled in, inspecting my liquor. Now *that* pissed me off. I don't play with my license—it was hard as hell to get. I sell top-shelf liquor. Yeah, there are a few cheaper brands, but not many. Bottom line—my shit is legit.

I sat at the bar watching as two inspectors tested my supply. When I saw them packing six bottles into a box, I had to step in.

"Look, man, ain't nothing wrong with that liquor. I just opened those bottles," I said calmly.

The motherfucker wasn't trying to hear it.

"This is procedure," he said. "We don't need your permission. If a bottle's open, we can take it. Owners always say nothing's wrong—until we check. You could've refilled it, watered it down. We've seen all kinds of shit. Read the policies. Sit tight—we'll be done shortly."

While this asshole was talking, my customers were still getting harassed.

Then the police walked up on *me*.

"Can I see your ID?" one asked as another whispered in his ear.

What the fuck is *that* about?

They ran my info and suddenly my name popped for an outstanding warrant.

What. The. Fuck?

"Stand up. Hands on your head," the cop ordered.

"What?"

"Hands behind your head, sir."

"Man, damn—what's going on?" I asked as he searched me.

Then he started reading my Miranda rights.

That's when I knew this shit was real.

"Man, I just opened this place—" I started.

"You can tell it to the judge," he snapped, cuffing me. "I'm just doing my job."

"To the judge? Damn, man—at least let me give my woman the keys. I can't leave the bar wide open."

Maya rushed over. "What's going on? Is he under arrest? Why are you arresting him?"

"Sergeant," the officer called out.

"Give her the keys," the sergeant said.

"Baby, I'm sorry," I told her. "You gotta lock the place up. Slice—"

"Come on," the officer barked.

"Hold up. Slice, help her manage the bar. Keep it open while I handle this. Make sure she gets home safe, aight?"

"I got it," Slice said. "Don't worry."

"I got this," Maya added, leaning against the bar.

They marched us outside, lined up, cuffs tight—like a damn chain gang. They came prepared for this shit.

I tried telling them they had the wrong person, but they weren't listening. I've never even had a speeding ticket.

Only explanation? Some bullshit. Mistaken identity—or Dice's bitch-ass stirring up trouble again.

I knew it.

The moment his ass walked in, I felt it.

I should've put his janky ass out the moment he walked through the door.

But no, listening to Pops, I was supposed to look out for my brother.

Same father, different mothers. We'd been raised in the same house since I was ten and he was twelve. From day one, it felt like he was always trying to one-up me. Always measuring himself against me.

That wasn't my fault.

Pops wasn't leaving my moms for his. He could've stayed with his own mother—trifling ass—knowing damn well Pops was already taken when she started fucking with him. And when Pops finally went home for good, she sent his ass right along with him. Didn't want him anymore because he reminded her too much of Pops.

That's the fucked-up part—he should've been grateful my moms took his ass in, knowing Pops had been creeping with his mother. But instead of gratitude, he brought resentment.

He was always in competition.

I never really understood why, but it was what it was. No matter how hard he tried, he could never outshine me. I listened when Pops talked. I took heed to his lessons—survival first, education always. He drilled that into me early: knowledge was the key, and discipline was how you used it.

Nobody, him included, ever thought I'd be shit. I was scrawny, quiet, and stayed to myself. When I left for college, I weighed a buck twenty-five soaking wet. When I came home, I was a solid, chiseled two-fifty—with skills.

They underestimated me for years. They thought I was a punk.

I guess I taught them a thing or two.

They took a good number of bikers from the club—Dice included—for one reason or another. I figured I'd be able to make bond, but they told me I had to appear before a judge in the morning. That's when I knew this wasn't going to be quick.

I recognized one of the officers and asked if I could use the phone. I needed to call Maya—needed to hear her voice and give her some direction. I didn't know how long it would take to straighten this bullshit out. He agreed.

I told her what happened and asked if she was comfortable handling the business until I got out. I needed her to contact my moms and Pops, let them know what was going on. I knew I could depend on her. Truth was, I just wanted to hear her voice, it grounded me.

We were still waiting to be processed. That shit took forever. The jail was crowded as hell, like they were giving something away. About ten of my crew got jammed up in this nonsense, along with members from other clubs.

I kept checking the clock, thinking how fucked up it was that I was sitting in jail without bail when I should've been laid up somewhere with Maya's fine ass. Cops were scurrying around, calling names for booking, and my irritation kept rising by the second.

"Hey, Deuce—they called your name," Spud yelled.

"Aight, man. Let me get this shit over with," I said, heading toward the door.

They called my name again.

"I'm coming. Damn."

Fingerprints. Mugshot. Body search. Cavity search.

That's when shit got weird.

My name and social came back in multiple cities and states—but my fingerprints didn't match any of it. I was hot. I knew exactly whose bullshit this was. Dice. Always fucking something up. I could understand why *he* was locked up—but why the fuck was I here?

After booking, a group of us were transferred to our cells.

To keep my sanity, I replayed moments with Maya—our nights together, her body, her smile. Thick, tight waist, that ass sitting just right. Those thoughts helped pass the time.

We were locked down for the weekend, pending court. Maya even sent a bondsman, but I still couldn't make bond because of an "ongoing investigation." Everything tied back to Dice and whatever dirt he'd been involved in.

It was cool, though. Some of my boys were there. I wasn't stressing—it was just a couple of days. I knew they had my back the same way I had theirs. I could hold my own.

One thing I knew for sure—I couldn't count on Dice.

That nigga wouldn't just throw me under the bus—he'd be driving it.

We went before the judge that Monday.

No bail.

The judge stated I had a parole violation and needed to report to my PO. I kept telling them they had the wrong man—that this was identity theft—but nobody was listening. The prosecutor claimed one of Dice's victims identified *me*. Me, of all people.

I was being held for a crime I never committed.

My lawyer immediately filed a brief requesting my release, but until the court sorted it out, I had to sit my ass down. I could see how the mistake happened, —Dice had used my Social Security number before during his criminal career. Hell, we damn near look like twins.

That shit pissed me off.

This was cutting into my money, my business, my life. The only good thing was being able to talk to Maya. She reassured me she had everything handled on the outside, and I trusted her.

They shipped us to Lorain and dropped us straight into General Population.

That place was nasty as fuck.

I couldn't understand why anyone would want to be a repeat offender. There was zero privacy. After another strip search, we stood there naked—grown men lined up like cattle. That's when I caught some fuck nigga staring at my dick.

What the fuck?

I guess some dudes compare other men's dicks—seeing who hangs low, who might be soft enough to get fucked. I don't know. I'm confident in mine, but I'm not interested in what another man's working with. That shit ain't for me. Whatever floats their boat—that's their business.

Standing there waiting on government-issued hand-me-downs, reality hit hard.

This shit was deep.

I went to jail humble—for something I didn't do—and nobody cared. All they knew was they had an *Andre Johnson* in custody. They also had *Andrez Johnson* locked up.

That was Dice.

His mama named him after my pops just to rub salt in shit, then he deliberately dropped the "z" whenever it benefited him. I don't know how he keeps getting away with it, but he does. Dice was just like his mama—no regard for anyone but himself.

It didn't help that we were born on the same damn day, two years apart.

Motherfuckers don't read.

Unfortunately, I wasn't bunked with my boys. Instead, I landed with a lifer named Raheem.

This cat had already done twenty-five years and still had a long road ahead of him. From what I'd heard about his reputation, when Raheem first came through these walls, he was *that dude*—cold-hearted, no conscience, nothing to play with. And even now, after all this time, he was still a cold motherfucka.

Raheem took Shahada his first month in. Islam grounded him.

His father had been a career criminal, spent time here and in other joints. One of his father's old associates took Raheem under his wing early on, and since then, he'd calmed down—at least on the surface. Inside these walls, he carried serious respect.

Make no mistake about it—he still wasn't someone to fuck with.

Some of the other motherfuckas in here needed religion *bad*. You ever hear that saying, *"Thank God for penitentiaries"*? Whoever coined that knew exactly what the fuck they were talking about. Some of these lifers didn't give a rat's ass about anyone back then—and some still don't give a fuck now.

Living in these abnormal conditions, I had to stay both hard *and* smart.

When I first walked into the cell, I held myself with confidence. I'd taken Shahada years ago and prayed five times a day for a stretch, so we already had common ground.

"As-salamu alaikum wa rahmatullah wa barakatuhu," I said.

"Wa 'alaykum as-salaam wa rahmatullah wa barakatuhu," he replied. "You Muslim?"

"I practiced in college… fell off my deen," I said.

"Insha'Allah, my brother," he nodded. "You'll find your path again."

I made my bed and laid down until they called us for dinner. I was looking forward to linking up with my boys. Raheem ate with the Muslim brothers—solid-looking men, the kind you didn't want problems with.

When I caught up with my crew, they already had the hookup in the kitchen. One thing is for sure—we weren't going to starve, even if the food was trash. We exchanged stories about our first few hours and our cellies. There's no real time to socialize in here—you eat, then it's back to your unit for count. That's it.

Day in and day out, the same routine.

Mail call, though—that was the highlight.

For a couple of weeks straight, I got letters from Maya every other day. That was the good shit. "Andre Johnson. Andre Johnson. Andre Johnson."

I felt special.

I always kept my letters on me—niggas in here were thirsty for mail, willing to rummage through your bunk if you let them. Maya's letters made for good night reading.

Other than that, jail was boring as hell.

Cards. Chess. TV.

The food sucked. The only things to look forward to were visitation, yard time with my boys, mail, and commissary.

You were told when to sleep, when to wake up, when to eat—damn near when to shit, shave, and bathe. If you want to talk about being pissed off, this was it. It felt like I was living inside a bad episode of *The Twilight Zone*.

Same bullshit on repeat.

Inmates playing cat and mouse with COs.

Niggas hustling each other.

Dudes looking for someone to fuck or get their dick sucked.

That was the routine.

I'd see Dice in the yard, but there wasn't much to say between us. Me and my boys stayed posse'd up in the weight pit, pumping iron. Body image mattered in here. With our lifestyle, you had to stay tight. There was always somebody looking to test you.

We didn't fuck with people—but we weren't the ones to be fucked with.

I stayed focused on my health, always had. Wearing a solid 250, six-pack carved, arms defined. Benching 250 easy, niggas stayed trying to figure out how someone built like me could rep the way I did. It wasn't size, it was muscle.

I finished my set and stood up to spot Spud when I noticed some niggas circling Dice.

Here we go again.

That nigga was *always* in some bullshit.

I watched for a minute. First blow landed. They squared up. One-on-one, it was cool. Fair.

But when others started inching in, trying to jump him—

Nah. That wasn't happening.

Even though we couldn't stand each other, Dice was still my brother. We might have beef, but ain't nobody gonna fuck with him. Pops would've been disappointed if I let something happen to him on my watch.

So, we moved.

One of the bullies—Trevor—turned toward me, puffed up. "What the fuck you got to do with this? I'm staking claim on my BITCH."

"I think you need to claim another BITCH," I snapped, pointing at Dice,

"'cause it won't be him, motherfucka'."

"Who the fuck is you?" he barked.

"Don't worry about who the fuck I am. Just know this one right here" I jabbed my finger again "will *never* be yours."

Trevor looked around at his boys.

"Who the fuck is this nigga to come in *my* house and tell me what I can and can't do? And who the fuck are *you* to tell me who I can claim as my bitch?"

I turned to Dice.

"You wanna be his bitch?" I asked.

"Hell naw!" Dice yelled. "The fuck I look like. These niggas don't want no work. I'll fuck you up—check my motherfuckin' record, bitch-ass nigga!"

"Hold up," I said, grabbing Dice's arm and pulling him back. "I got this."

Then I looked dead at Trevor.

"When a man tells you he doesn't want to be bothered with your ass, you leave him the fuck alone. This is my brother—and ain't nobody doing a motherfuckin' thing to him. Not today. Not ever."

We started walking off.

Raheem came over with a couple of brothers.

"Everything good, Deuce?" he asked calmly.

"These silly motherfuckas trying to claim what belongs to me," I said.

Raheem shook his head, pointing at Trevor's crew.

"I don't like them niggas anyway. Shaytan all over 'em. Straight devils."

That's when Trevor's boy lunged at me—with a shank.

Spud caught that nigga with a mean uppercut, followed by a clean two-piece. That gave me just enough time to drop another chump with a gut shot and a knockout.

Raheem and his crew jumped in.

It was on and poppin'.

Dice stepped up, and we were whoopin' ass. Straight stomping niggas out. The yard exploded into chaos.

Guards flooded the place with gas.

The Goon Squad rushed in wearing riot gear.

Saved by the bell.

We weren't bullshittin'. We were laying damage.

Aftermath?

Some of us went straight to the hole.

A few got shipped to another pod.

One of Raheem's boys got sent to max—he was headed there anyway. That nigga had a real violent history. Crushing people type shit.

Here I go again, getting into shit because of this nigga. If the shoe were on the other foot, I doubt he'd do the same for me. Probably not. Damn.

They escorted us to the hole and locked us down in a cell barely bigger than my regular one—except this one was built for isolation. Barely any light. Or maybe it just felt that way. Even the glow from the small glass window was dim at best. This was some dark-ass shit.

I was pissed like a motherfucker. Couldn't believe I'd gotten myself pulled into more bullshit. I tried to calm down, lying back with my eyes closed, forcing myself to visualize Maya.

That's when it hit me.

They'd taken her letters out of my pockets before throwing me in the hole.

One thing they couldn't take, though, was what I carried in my mind—her touch, her smile, the sound of her laughter, and most of all, her love. Even without her here physically, I felt her presence. I'd read her letters so many times that her words were etched into my memory—into my heart.

Solitary confinement taught me the true meaning of loneliness. I'd never felt like this before. But her words gave me something these walls couldn't take—freedom. When you're free, you don't always realize how important it is to have someone who genuinely cares about you. Too often, that kind of love gets taken for granted.

I was lucky. I had Maya.

After a few days, they walked me back to general population. As I was heading toward my cell, I crossed paths with Saboor—one of Raheem's crew. We couldn't talk long with staff nearby.

"Deuce," he said quietly, "Raheem sent his salaams. He said to chill. We got your back."

"Thanks, brother," I replied. "Salaamu Alaikum."

Raheem caught a couple more days than I did. I figured he would. During the chaos, he'd roughed up a few COs—not intentionally. When they tried restraining him, they got in the way as he went after one of Trevor's boys. He swung, missed his target, and slammed a CO into the wall. I probably wouldn't see him for a while.

I grabbed clean clothes and got ready for chow. Me and Spud were talking through the incident when count was called. We had to return to our bunks.

After count, I laid back and pulled out a letter from Maya.

Maya's Letter (edited for flow, voice preserved):

Hey My Somebody,

I miss you.

I stopped by to see your folks. They're holding it together, worried, but good. They ask about you like you're just out on a long ride and not somewhere they can't reach.

I know it's only been a little over a week, but I already miss your presence. The way you'd pull me close at night, how safe it felt lying against you until sleep took over.

I keep replaying our first night together. The way you took your time with me. The way you made me forget everything outside that room. Just thinking about it still makes my body respond to you.

When you read this, breathe me in. I pressed a little of my perfume into the paper, so you won't forget my scent. I want you to remember how I sound when I want you, how my body reacts to yours.

I can't wait until you come home so I can remind you in person.

Until then, keep me close.

Remember that bay! I miss the shit out of you. I can't wait until you get home so I can see you. Here is a picture of what I am like when I think of you. I drip for you.

Have a good night...next letter with more.

Love You! Maya

After reading Maya's letter, my dick was hard. Jacking off while staring at her picture, I imagined her legs gapped, pussy wet, my dick buried deep inside her. Damn, I missed the fuck out of her. I couldn't wait to get home and fuck her again.

Once I busted my nut, I took a long whiff of her perfume before folding the letter back up. I kissed her picture, then closed my eyes.

Morning came fast. I ate, handled my business, and headed back to my cell. I pulled the rest of her letters from my pocket and started reading. The Jones was back—and this time it was worse. Her words stayed with me, crawling under my skin. My dick stayed hard, and I was constantly adjusting myself just from thinking about her.

Walking around with that kind of tension wasn't smart either. I didn't want anybody getting the wrong impression—or me having to whip somebody's ass over it. Truth was, not getting no pussy made me mean. Sometimes jacking off was the only thing keeping me balanced.

If I wasn't in the shower and didn't have lotion or Vaseline, I had to improvise. When I was sent to the hole, there was nothing. No lube, no comfort—just Maya's pictures and my imagination. I did what I had to do. Palmalina and her five friends—fuck four, I needed all the help I could get.

Pre-cum only worked for so long. Soap did the trick, but the dryness made shit rough. Still, I made it work.

I needed to get the fuck out of here and get some real pussy. Just looking at her picture made me hard, especially when I was alone. I thought about the first time we fucked. I was tired as hell and hadn't had pussy in forever—but none of that mattered. Pressure will bust a pipe.

For two days straight, I jacked my dick raw. Sex is physical and psychological—you need both. One without the other ain't enough. Stud slid me some hooch, which didn't help the situation. Shit just made it worse. Every thought of her naked, her thick ass riding me, had me heated all over again.

I couldn't remember what day it was—just that I'd been here long enough to count meals instead of time. My mind was starving for conversation. My body was starving for her touch.

No matter how hard I got looking at her pictures, I couldn't keep jacking off. It felt like I was rubbing my skin off. Spit and everything else stopped working. Push-ups and sit-ups became my escape—kept my body tight and my mind off fucking.

Dinner came, and I wasn't hungry. I was horny. But discipline mattered, so I ate anyway. When I glanced at the dessert section, the creaminess of the applesauce set my mind wandering. I took some back with me.

Later that night, I pulled out her picture again.

I made do with what I had.

Chapter Seven

Taboo

Make no mistake about it—I know the difference between making love and fucking. I wasn't discriminating. If it had to be one or the other, at least do it right. I've had past sexual encounters that were just plain ole boring. Basic missionary, flat-on-your-back kind of fuckin'. Shit, if I was lucky, I'd get fucked from the back while lying on my stomach.

When he finished, he was finished. No after-play. No nothing. It was very seldom that I bust. I didn't even have to fake like the sex was good. As long as he was on top, grinding and getting his nut, he was all right. And I was just left there unsatisfied, with a wet ass. Unfulfilled, I'd go home and play with my toys.

Having my toys as a backup, I knew I was guaranteed to cum at least one, two, maybe three times. Self-satisfaction was the icing on the cake— and I do like my cake.

Talk about the luck of the draw—it's fucked up that the last three niggas I dated had really lame fuck game. What the fuck? I know I'm slipping. This shit makes me want to go back and holla at AJ. Man, did he have a nice dick—and he knew exactly what to do with it. There was nothing lame about our sex life. He loved to eat pussy, and I loved to suck his dick. But as luck would have it, he's married now. I guess my unwillingness to get married cost me that relationship. So needless to say, I've been stuck with some bullshit.

Each partner I encountered brought more and more to the table, but it still wasn't ride-or-die dick, if you know what I mean. It was like I was being spoon-fed what *they* wanted me to have during the experience, with no consideration for what *I* needed.

For a minute, I became complacent. Sex was just that—unfulfilling. Boring. I knew when it was all said and done, there was still the crème de la crème: my goody bag. One hundred percent guaranteed satisfaction. I knew what I needed—no mystery about it. The toys were winning.

Well… not so fast. Something was still missing. Shit, if it wasn't for the need to be held—to feel a nigga lying on top of me—I could be content at home. But every now and then, I needed that human contact to bring some real excitement back into my life.

After I met him, he flipped the script by eliminating the monotony. My sex life went from a ho-hum experience to an undeniably satisfying one. He opened the door and got me hooked by seducing me mentally, so to speak. The grass was definitely greener on the other side of the fence.

He unleashed the beast I knew lived within me, the same beast AJ once tapped into and the one my toys only flirted with. I realized I needed more, and it was time to fulfill my sexual desires. The freak was reborn.

Chapter One – The Meeting

I first saw Pooch at Dap's Memorial Day Weekend Potluck and Cookout. Dawn and I met up with Tiff, Jenn, and Kels outside to make sure we were presentable before making our grand entrance. Clothes straight, not a strand of hair out of place, no lipstick on our teeth—the normal girl shit you do before hitting a spot full of niggas. It was just a habit we developed when we went out.

Even though we knew Dap and his boys, we still had our reputation to protect. Besides, who knew who we might run into?

Since this was a potluck, we brought dishes to share. We didn't want the meal to consist of just barbecue and somebody's store-prepared food. There was no contest, but bragging rights were part of the fun. So, of course, we strutted in with food in hand—foxy and turning heads.

We dropped our dishes at the potluck table, made our rounds, spoke to the guests, then retreated to our favorite area. The place was packed. As usual, there were niggas there I had never seen before. That was one of the best parts of Dap's cookouts—meeting new people, especially the men. It was time to Nancy Drew that ass. Me and my girls knew how to work it.

We sat there pointing out everyone we thought was fuckable. Unbelievably, there wasn't one duck in sight. Most sets I go to have at least one ugly ass duck lurking around, trying—and usually failing—to spit game.

Feeling nice after sipping my second cup of Hunch Punch, I became more attentive. Dap's Hunch Punch was like drinking a Kamikaze, except it was made with multiple liquors of different proofs. That's why he called it Hunch Punch—you never knew how many alcohols you were about to digest. All you knew was that if you didn't pace yourself, the liquor would sneak up and punch the shit out of you.

Talking about getting smashed, I'd had my share. Shit started moving in slow motion. I was catching everything. A nigga couldn't get nothing past me. My senses went into overdrive, which sparked my curiosity.

Who was the fourth wheel standing with Dap, Sly, and Los? I mean… his ass was fine. I *needed* to know who he was.

"Yo, who the fuck is that?" I blurted out.

"Who?" Dawn asked.

"Him—Tyrese's brother," I said jokingly.

"Man, what the fuck? Tyrese's brother? For real? What the fuck are you talking about?" she said. "He doesn't look shit like Tyrese. You trippin'."

"Midnight in the burgundy Aeropostale shirt," I said, pointing toward Dap.

"You stupid," Dawn said. "That's Pooch—Dap's cousin. And stop pointing."

"Where the fuck did he come from? I've never seen him before," I said.

"He just moved here from down south," Dawn replied.

"Damn, that nigga look good as fuck to me right now—his chocolate tan glimmering in the sun."

"You want me to introduce you?" Dawn asked.

"Hell yeah!"

"I gotchu," she said, giving me a thumb-up.

It was time to break bread. Plates were on chug—plenty to go around, and nobody was holding back.

"Damn, this mac and cheese is slamming. Let me get a little more of that," Pooch belted.

My girls turned around acting stupid, pointing at me and over my head. With my mouth full, I shot them a condescending look like, *I know my shit is bad.* With their loud asses, there was no way he didn't know I made it.

He pointed in my direction, nodded in approval, and said, "Girl, you put your foot in this. It's the bomb."

He went back to talking with his boys while I sat there getting clowned by my friends.

"Now you know what they say—food is the path to a man's dick," Kels said jokingly, as everyone laughed.

"It's heart, not dick, Kels," I said, almost choking on my food.

"No, if you feed a man right, you *get* the dick," she said with a smirk.

"Girl, shut up—you're crazy!" I hollered, pushing her shoulder. I laughed so hard tears came to my eyes. We were having big fun.

Niggas were stuffed. Conversations picked back up, chairs scraped, and people pushed away from the table. Plates were cleared and everyone went back to mingling.

I was good—full as fuck, stomach on pop. I ducked off into the cut to unbutton my pants. A sista needed a breather. Pulling my shirt down, I thought, *Damn, I knew I shouldn't have been trying to act cute.*

I turned around and ran smack into Pooch.

"Excuse me," I said, slightly embarrassed.

"Twink?" he said.

"Yeah," I replied, smoothing my shirt. *I hope he didn't see that trifling ass shit,* I thought.

"I was looking for you," he said.

"Me... why?" I asked, my voice betraying the butterflies in my stomach.

"I wanted to introduce myself—and find out when you were inviting me over for dinner."

"Dinner? Why would I do that? I don't know you," I said, trying to be hard, knowing damn well I didn't mind his boldness.

"My name's Pooch," he said, extending his hand.

"I don't know you like that, to be inviting you to my house."

"You can get to know me. I'm Dap's cousin—he said you good people. That's all I need to know. Plus, that million-dollar smile and your cooking?" He smiled. "You know what they say about the path to a man's heart."

Oh no, he did not just go there, I thought.

"Look, I just moved to town," he continued. "I don't know many females outside of family. Hope you don't mind me being so forward. I'd really like to get to know you. So... how about it?"

Chapter Two – Courting Phase

We exchanged phone numbers and chatted damn nearly every night. Our conversations were stimulating, and we had a lot in common. One thing he enjoyed was playing cards—and I loved a good game myself. Playing cards were right up my alley. He preferred Bid Whist over Spades.

Not to mention, he was a big movie buff. I loved watching movies, so that worked too. So far, I found him interesting.

We began seeing each other every now and then—nothing serious at first. But as time passed, we started spending more and more time together, even going on out-of-town rendezvous. On one trip, he took me to meet his parents.

For six months, we kicked it. We had grown accustomed to each other's company. Keeping it real—we were boo'd up.

It was time for things to become more intimate. Not physically, but mentally. I already had the physical; now I was craving mental stimulation. Night after night, he made love to my psyche, massaging my internal state of mind with his words, his attention, and his presence.

I began falling.

Never had a man stimulated me this way—well, not in a long time anyway. I was wide open.

And I couldn't help but wonder… what was next?

Chapter Three – The Hook, Line, and Sinker

Just about every weekend, we played cards—jumping from house to house, whoever's turn it was to host. Bid Whist was the game of choice, though every now and then someone wanted to play Spades. Seven and out.

This weekend, the game landed at my house. Pooch was the perfect host. Women versus the men were the terms—and of course, we won. Everyone on my team is a winner. I don't know why they keep coming for me. They can't see me at the table, no matter how hard they try.

When everyone left, he helped clean up. We finished a little after 2:00 a.m., and I was beat down. I made it to the couch, kicked my feet up, and closed my eyes. Seeing how exhausted I was, he started massaging my feet.

With the lights down low, he placed my foot in his lap and ran his fingers between my toes, pressing into the ball of my foot. Man—did he know all the right pressure points. As he worked my feet, my body relaxed. I'd heard of acupressure, but I had no idea my body would respond like *this*.

The gentle pressure sent a tingling sensation straight to my vagina. And it didn't stop there. When he started manipulating the muscles in my calves, it was on. A warm, ravaging feeling spread through my body. I rested my foot against his dick. The more I rubbed it, the more heightened my jones became.

The evening had started with a good game of cards among friends. Now, it was clearly headed toward hot, passionate sex. *This should be interesting.*

I leaned forward, unzipped his pants, and pulled his dick out. Pooch bent down, kissing me passionately. I continued to rub him as he pushed me back onto the couch and started rubbing my pussy through my pants. After pulling his off, he slowly helped me out of mine. When he finished, I grabbed the throw blanket from the arm of the chair and spread it across the couch.

I laid back. Hovering over me—one knee on the couch, the other foot on the floor—I grabbed his dick and took the head into my mouth.

His lips found my clit, his tongue stroking and pressing, moving side to side until it hardened beneath his touch.

Grabbing my leg, he lifted my hips slightly and buried his tongue inside my pussy, sucking up my juices. As he licked and sucked, my clit twitched and my vagina began to contract. The sensation kept building, climbing higher, like a release waiting to explode. I was right on the edge—ready to bust—when he stopped.

It was like he knew exactly when I was about to cum and how to pull back without killing the mood.

Feeling how thick his dick was in my mouth, I imagined what it would feel like inside me. The excitement had him locked in. He moved me onto my knees, positioning me for doggy style. At that point, it was obvious—this sex was not going to be boring. Not by any stretch of imagination.

There was plenty of room for me to settle onto the couch as he lined up behind me. Already wet from anticipation, his entrance was smooth. Slow and steady, he rocked into me, cupping one of my breasts in his hand. Our bodies found a rhythm, moving together as one.

He pulled out and rotated the head of his dick around my opening before thrusting back in, deeper this time. Without missing a beat, he picked up the pace. His words were hot and low in my ear as he talked through his pleasure. I could feel his balls slapping against my body as he pounded my pussy.

"You like this dick? Give me that pussy—give it to me. Cum for me. You ready?" he said, pumping faster and harder.

"You know this pussy good, don't you?" I gasped, fighting for air. "Is the pussy good? You like this pussy?" I was feeling myself and had no problem saying it.

He hit the spot, and his body went into full convulsions. "Yeah… yeah… ooooh… ahhh," he moaned.

We collapsed, lifeless, with him lying against my back. Breathing heavy, he kissed down my spine before rolling over and drifting into a deep sleep. I cuddled up next to him, adrenaline still coursing through my body, releasing a satisfied sigh.

The sex had been incredible.

Chapter Four – The Cup Cake Phase

For the next couple of months, we were inseparable. Wherever I was seen, he was right there. He courted the fuck out of me. Just because he'd send gifts and flowers—either to my house or my job. Sometimes he'd surprise me with lunch. He was a romantic.

If I had to describe it, my heart was the target, and his arrow was aimed straight at the bull's-eye. And I loved it.

We were genuinely having a good time. One of the most important things about our relationship was the openness we developed. Being on the same page sexually made everything easier. Our sex life had reached another level. We explored role-playing, acting out different characters in different scenarios. Over time, I'd played a secretary, a maid, a waitress— and even a policewoman.

Whenever I hear Lil' Wayne's *Mrs. Officer*, shit… I get flashbacks and instantly get wet.

… When I get up all in ya (yeah)

We can hear the angels calling us (chea)

We can see the sunrise before us (yeah)

And when I'm in that thing, I'll make that body sang

(she know what I mean) I make it say

Wee ooh wee ooh wee (wee),

Wee ooh wee ooh wee (wee),

Wee ooh wee ooh wee,

(like a cop car)…

Talking about fun—we truly enjoyed each other's company. He was extremely supportive of my career. Anytime I had a business presentation coming up, he became my sounding board—listening as I practiced, coaching me through my delivery, and critiquing me when needed. He had become my number one cheerleader.

That morning, I woke up anxious, knowing I had a major presentation to give to my board members and several big investors. I'd worked hard to get where I was and wanted to make a strong impression. Briefcase in hand and dressed to kill, I walked into the office nickel sharp. After the previous night's sexcapade, I grabbed a vanilla latte to keep myself alert.

I didn't want to leave Pooch, but obligations are obligations, it's called having a job. Taking off wasn't an option. Still, I couldn't wait to get home and pick up where we left off. My sex life was the bomb. No more complacency—those days were officially over.

I had prepped the executive boardroom the day before, and arriving two hours early gave me time to settle in. I placed my coffee and briefcase on the conference table, then realized I'd left several files in my office.

When I returned to the boardroom and walked toward the whiteboard, I heard the door close—and then the lock clicked.

Startled, I turned around. There he stood, stroking his dick.

"How did you get in here?" I asked.

"The secretary said you'd just arrived and that I could go to the back," he said. "I told her I had a surprise for you. I guess she's so used to me bringing gifts, she didn't want to ruin it by calling you."

What could I say? He had a way of making grand entrances—and I didn't mind this early-morning visit at all. As he kissed me, flashes of last night rushed through my mind. A warm sensation settled low in my stomach as my coochie responded in anticipation of some taboo shit.

If this was about spicing things up, the risk was worth it.

I rushed to close the blinds, catching the seductive look in his eyes. Some serious business was about to happen in that room—and it had nothing to do with my presentation. As he kissed me, I felt his hard dick pressing against my body. I grabbed his hand and dragged him to the executive chair, pushing him down.

With my skirt hiked up, I positioned myself in front of him while he stroked himself. That was all the invitation I needed. I leaned in and went to work, carefully caressing his head with my tongue, licking and flicking it ravenously. He grabbed my head, guiding the motion slowly, deliberately. I could tell he was close.

I was in my groove—fully locked in. If he hadn't thought about being in love before, he was about to learn today. *All right, all right, all right,* I thought in my Kevin Hart voice.

He pushed me back while jacking his dick, forcing my head down until I gagged. As his body gyrated, he released, and I swallowed every drop.

Checking the clock, I realized time was moving fast. In less than ninety minutes, I'd be standing in front of a room full of people presenting my project. Panties soaked, I stepped out of them and tossed them onto the conference table. I climbed up, one foot on a chair, the other resting against his leg.

He slid between my thighs and went to work, licking my clit as I scooted forward to get every bit of it. He ate my pussy like a boss, manipulating my clit with his tongue and lips until my body responded. Pulling me off the table, he guided me to the windowsill. Bent over, gripping the ledge, I felt his dick rub against my ass before he lined himself up.

Already wet, he slid in easily. Inch by inch, I felt the need to flex and squeeze—those Kegel exercises paying off. Pulling out slowly, leaving just the head inside, he thrust forward again, deeper this time.

"Bam, bam, bam. Take this dick," he said. "This my pussy, huh? This my pussy?"

The pressure built relentlessly. My clit twitched on and off until the sensation erupted. Waves of pleasure radiated through my body, electricity branching outward as my muscles convulsed. My entire body tightened as I climaxed—and he followed right behind me, gripping my waist as he reached his peak.

The only downside to taboo sex on the job was that it had to end. He had to leave. I had to work.

With thirty minutes to spare, he slipped out the same way he'd come—in desire and heat. My body felt amazing, my mind clear and focused. This presentation was going to be a piece of cake.

I sprayed the room with lavender neutralizer, wiped down the desk and chair, then rushed to the restroom for a quick hoe bath and to straighten my clothes. As soon as I returned to the boardroom, the phone rang. The secretary let me know guests were arriving.

Moments later—*bzzz, bzzz.*

"Hello?" I answered.

It was Pooch.

"I know you're busy," he said. "Thanks for breakfast—you were good as always. Hope I helped take the edge off. Have a great presentation. See you after work. XoXoXo."

My nose was wide. Just the thought of him—and that dick—sent chills through my body. That was a full-body orgasm if I'd ever had one.

Some might call it sickening.

I called it Taboo.

And I was enjoying myself.

Chapter Five – Addiction

Now, I know what a damn addict feels like. When that Jones hit you, you got to go! On the real, I was addicted to this man. Yeah, I mean that man knows how to work that dick! He had me open, I knew it and so did everybody else! I think it took me every bit of our courtship for the feelings to overtake me. After he upped his fuck game, it was on. Now that we are in this cupcake phase, we have become inseparable. These last encounters have sky-rocketed me to a whole different level. I was in love!

I could tell that he was becoming more relaxed in our relationship. He started leaving shit every time he came over to the house. First, it was a shirt, then it was some socks and shoes; later, his draws wound up in the laundry. At some point, not sure when, but he began occupying several dresser drawers and space in my closet. He was over damn nearly every day. I really didn't mind, not one bit. In fact, I started thinking that it might only be right, at this point, for him to move in. I just had to figure out the right time to make that suggestion. I just had to figure out the right time to ask.

I know he has a life outside of me. And I didn't want to necessarily push him into deciding he wasn't ready to make. He was already halfway in, may as well come all the way. I am a gambling person, the worst he can say is no! Tonight, I was going to test the waters. I cooked one of his favorite dishes. I waited until he finished his meal, then I popped the question while he was watching Bad Boys 2 for the umpteenth time. Well, he accepted with no reservations. That weekend he moved what appeared to be the rest of his stuff, which wasn't much. Most of his shit was here already. I believe moving in was his intention, anyway. Afterward, we celebrated our decision. With the combination of alcoholic beverages, good food, and his sexy ass, that sealed the deal. The evening ended in a state of ecstasy.

Chapter Six – No Need To Lie

When he moved up from the South, he landed a nice-ass job working for a consulting firm. Come to think of it, I don't even remember the firm's name. It had some weird-ass pronunciation. That's crazy as fuck, now that I think about it. I guess I never really pressed him about it. All I knew was that when payday came, bills got paid.

For real, I didn't even have to work if I didn't want to.

Some nights, he stayed out late. Having worked in corporate myself, I knew long hours came with the territory. I'd had plenty of late nights of my own, so I didn't trip when he said he had to work over. He shared bits and pieces about his job responsibilities, but there were certain things he stayed tight-lipped about. I chalked it up to confidentiality.

Still… something always felt off.

Whenever he talked about work-related situations, it seemed like pieces were missing. Like he was paid not to disclose certain details, especially when it came to the large incentives he received. The way he spoke made it clear it was a need-to-know situation, and I only needed to know what *he* decided to tell me.

What I *did* know was that his pay fluctuated. One time, he won a five-day, all-expenses-paid trip to the Eastern Caribbean. He showered me with gifts regularly, like it was nothing. On occasion, he'd have evening functions where he entertained clients.

Some nights, he'd come in reeking of liquor and cheap dollar-store fragrances.

He swore there was no cheating going on. But what he *didn't* do was explain what the fuck *was* going on. The crazy part was that his commission checks always justified the unaccounted-for time. So, I let it slide... until I couldn't.

One evening, he called to say he wasn't coming home for dinner. A client had come into town unexpectedly, and he was the one chosen. That night, he crept in late smelling like liquor and knockoff Issey Miyake.

I didn't want to think the worst, but sometimes your mind plays tricks on you. None of it made sense. I was feeling some type of way— call it jealousy or whatever the fuck you want.

"Sleep yo' bitch ass on the couch," I yelled, slinging a pillow at him.

"Baby don't do that. Let me explain."

"Explain?" I snapped. "Explain *what*? You mean explain why you've been gone for hours and came back smelling like a five-dollar hooker?"

"More like a five-hundred-dollar hooker," he mumbled under his breath.

"What?"

"Baby, just let me explain."

"For real—you really don't want to talk to me right now," I said coldly. "I have zero understanding in this moment. So I suggest you get some sleep and try this shit again tomorrow."

I turned toward the window.

"I'm sleeping in the guest room. Fuck a couch," he muttered. "Who the fuck are you to be kicking me out of my bed? That's some bitch shit."

With that, he walked into the adjacent room, closing the door behind him.

Chapter Seven – Part Time

As the end of the fiscal year approached Pooch's job, his hours grew longer. Because I only *half* trusted the situation, I didn't call—but I did wonder what the fuck was really going on. When he came home, he was exhausted most nights, heading straight to the shower. *Trying to wash her off,* I thought.

I was determined to find out the truth. Before I put his ass out, I needed to know if I had something to worry about. I'd invested too much into this relationship to let it go down the drain without answers.

But first, I wanted him to feel what I was feeling.

I started staying out late on the nights he *was* home. Let him wonder—since I was being kept in the dark. I was a single woman only on the nights I went out. If he was doing him, then I was going to do me. And I was good at keeping secrets.

It didn't take long for him to notice. His attitude shifted. He started spending more time at home, working fewer late nights, no longer missing in action. One thing that never changed, though, was the role-play during sex. That part of our relationship wasn't suffering at all.

If sex were my only yardstick, I wouldn't have had a leg to stand on—I was getting mine. But then again, that didn't mean he wasn't getting his rocks off somewhere else. It was the unaccounted-for hours that kept my suspicions alive.

He became more attentive around the house—doing things for me the way he did earlier in the relationship, before the honeymoon phase wore off. Maybe he missed me. Maybe he felt the shift. Withholding attention was part of the game.

Make no mistake about it—I didn't withhold the pussy.

That evening, we planned to spend some quality time at home. I noticed he kept brushing against my ass, all touchy-feely. He was definitely feeling horny, and I wasn't mad at it. Pulling out our *Fuck List*, he scanned for any roles or places we hadn't explored yet.

Keeping a list was our way of keeping things spicy. We'd gotten real creative—always finding new ways to fuck. Spontaneity mattered just as much as planning, like that taboo sex in the conference room. After that day, we added it to the list of approved locations. Pooch had a gift for pulling the freak out of me.

Tonight, he decided the pool would be perfect—an eighty-degree evening, streetlights glowing, the night quiet. We stripped naked and headed outside. Moonlight danced across the still water. Pooch sat on the edge of the pool, feet dangling in as I poured the wine.

He suggested I grab one of my toys.

Leaving him there, I ran upstairs to my room and pulled my goody bag from the toy chest. While I was gone, his phone beeped. Curiosity got the best of me.

I checked the text.

Meet and greet.

8:00 p.m. tomorrow.

Winchester Hotel – Penthouse Suite, Euclid Avenue.

Commission: $1,000.

Well… well… well. *This is some interesting shit.*

I grabbed my bag, placed his phone back exactly where it was, and headed downstairs—ready for Water Wonderland. Pushing the bullshit out of my head so it wouldn't completely ruin the mood, I sat on the edge of the pool and spread my legs.

He looked energized, showing off as he swam laps back and forth. Watching him move through the water was surprisingly stimulating—the strength in his arms, the power in his legs slicing through the pool. Funny how something so simple could feel so sensual.

He stood at a distance, locked eyes with me, then dove back in— swimming straight toward me. As he reached me, he rose slowly, splashing water in a teasing, ritualistic way. Moonlight shimmered across his body, highlighting every muscle. Sexual energy radiated from him, thick and undeniable.

Just watching him made my pussy swell.

His appetite was voracious. He went down on me with the same intensity he'd shown in the water. His tongue attacked my clit, sending waves of pleasure crashing through my body. In my mind, the splashing water mirrored the sensations—bigger splashes, deeper pleasure. His tongue felt like some mystical wand, triggering powerful explosions inside me.

Slowing down, he slipped a finger inside my pussy, then brought it to his mouth, tasting me like ambrosia. My clit was hard—I was close. Sliding into the pool, I leaned back against the jets. The water became his element.

He fucked me stupid.

Each thrust sent waves rippling across the surface, turning the calm pool into chaos—like a tsunami after an earthquake. When he hit that spot, my orgasm went off the Richter scale. My body convulsed, clit pulsing violently as pleasure ripped through me in seismic waves.

When it was over, the water settled. My pussy twitched as the contractions slowly faded.

Pooch kissed me and leaned against the side of the pool before swimming back toward the center, splashing water across his chest like he was showing off. Maybe he was.

I got the message.

That water action was everything.

Damn… I loved this nigga.

Chapter Eight – Do Me

To execute my plan, I had to enlist the help of my girls. It had been a minute since we'd done anything this calculated—and mischievous. Operation Winchester was officially underway. I left the house with one goal in mind: to fuck some shit up.

I was styled in a blue schoolgirl skirt, striped thigh-highs, and a crisp white button-up blouse. My bang fell perfectly across my forehead, hair swooped and pinned up with chopsticks. I looked like a thick Powerpuff Girl—cute but grown.

Heads turned the moment we entered the room. Our presence demanded attention; that's just how we move. Along with the stares came the chatter. Thinking back to my single days, this venue would've been a gold mine—prospects everywhere. Champagne bottles popped, and everybody was dressed to kill.

Then the lights dimmed.

Perfect timing.

Everyone took their seats, and so did we. *When in Rome…* The auctioneer stepped up and announced the bidding was about to begin.

"Welcome, ladies and gentlemen. This evening was designed with you in mind. Each participating company has listed their most prized employees in the catalog—individuals you'll have the opportunity to sit down with. Invitations were sent out with RSVPs required. As you can see, the room is divided into sections—participants here, spectators there. Once the auction concludes and payments are complete, we'll enjoy a magnificent meal courtesy of our master chef from ETC Cuisine. Bidding will begin at a minimum of $5,000. May the highest bidder win."

The first man hit the stage in a sharp Hugo Boss suit, wing tips shining.

"Ladies, this is Mr. Jones from Stone Basics Accounting Firm. He specializes in pushing all the right buttons," the auctioneer said.

We exchanged looks.

"Well… this just got interesting," I whispered.

We watched quietly as women bid on their company's choice—*man*. Then Pooch stepped onto the stage, dressed in a black Tom Ford suit, pink button-down, and black bow tie.

Now I *knew* something was up.

The bidding started at $5,000 and immediately turned into a war between two women. Paddles flew. The price climbed to $15,000.

Damn. They were bidding on these men like cattle. Modern-day slavery.

Then one woman called out, "Thirty thousand."

"Do I hear thirty-three?" the auctioneer asked.

Silence.

"Thirty thousand—going once, going twice… sold to the lady in black!"

Pooch stepped off the stage as the next man entered. And just like that, it clicked. *Now I see how he affords the luxuries.*

Once bidding wrapped up, people mingled before moving to the dining area. Just like the auction, seating was divided. I spotted Pooch seated with the woman who'd won him, a waiter taking their order.

Business talk, I assumed—until she started leaning in, touching his thigh.

That was my cue.

I walked over to slow that shit *all* the way down.

For $30,000, what exactly did she think she bought?

When Pooch looked up and realized it was me, his face cracked. Shocked didn't even begin to cover it.

"Excuse me," I said smoothly. "Can I borrow him for a hot second? I'll return him—we just need to settle a little business."

I grabbed his hand and pulled him up. Professional. Calm. Controlled.

He fucked me at *my* place of employment, so it only felt right that I fucked him at *his*.

As I walked away, she mouthed, *Bitch.*

I thought, *yeah. A good bitch. And this one's mine.*

I knew him—what made him tick, how to push him, how to turn him on. One of his weaknesses had always been beautiful women. That's how he got me. And watching him with her told me everything I needed to know.

I pulled him into the ladies' room and locked the door.

My tongue was down his throat before his back hit the wall. I slid my hand into my panties, stroked my pussy, and pushed my fingers into his mouth. Feeling the heat, he spun me around and lifted me onto the sink.

He parted my legs and went to work—licking, sucking, finger-fucking me exactly how I liked it. The thrill of possibly getting caught had me hotter than the Fourth of July.

"I'm about to cum," I whispered.

He unzipped his pants, stroking himself as I wrapped my legs around him. He rubbed the head of his dick up and down my clit until he was fully hard, then thrust inside me.

Ah-ha.

He kissed my neck, nibbled my ear, breathing heavy as the pressure built. When he finally came, my body melted completely as we held each other, kissing slow and deep.

I climbed down, sucking the salt of my juices from his tongue before we cleaned up.

A knock came at the door.

"Hello? Is someone in there?" the maître d' called.

"Just a moment," I replied.

Pooch smirked like he was about to say something slick. I covered his mouth, stifling laughter.

"Just a moment," I repeated.

Once we stepped into the hallway, he slipped back and tipped her generously. She gave me a nod and a thumbs-up of approval.

Back in the dining room, the highest bidder waited patiently. I apologized for the delay and thanked her for her patience—and for supporting the company.

Before I walked away, I leaned into Pooch's ear.

"There's more of that waiting for you at home," I whispered. "Bon appétit."

Chapter Eight
Mind Blow

As a habit, when I go to sleep at night, I close my bedroom door. I'm not sure where I picked up this behavior, but I think I've watched too many damn horror movies. For some reason, the thought of someone—or something—walking past my door, peering in on me, let alone coming through it, creeps me out.

In my mind, closing the door prevents any possible contact with creepy shit invading my space—especially anything fucking with my head. I know what you're thinking: a grown-ass man afraid of the dark and believing a door can shield him from whatever lurks in the night.

That theory was disproven the night she opened the door and stood before me.

Her thick, statuesque body approached my bed as I struggled to get a clear view of what she was. The scariest part? The door closed behind her. She glided forward, stopping just short of my footboard. Her sheer covering cascaded to the floor at her feet.

I wanted desperately to sit up and see her, but I couldn't move. Paralyzed—trapped in some twilight state, I lay there waiting for something terrible to happen. Her airy appearance made it impossible to see any facial features. Shit… for that matter, I couldn't even tell *what* she was.

I fought like hell to use my limbs, but nothing worked.

She slid the covers off me, climbed on top, and straddled my body. Heat rushed through me when she lightly kissed and sucked my neck and chest. Even with her so close, I still couldn't make out her face. It scared the shit out of me—and at the same time, it turned me on.

My adrenaline surged. Inch by inch, I felt my dick harden until it stood at full erection. This was some truly freaky shit.

She lifted herself and sank back down, my dick sliding into her pussy. A warm, silky sensation enveloped me as she gyrated in my lap. Her hands pressed against my chest as her body bucked like she was riding a mechanical bull. She moved in every direction while my body followed her rhythm. Her juices coated me as she swerved her hips, riding me hard and steady.

It felt so good that I fought my invisible restraints until they finally released me. Still unable to see her face, she made sure I *felt* her presence. I gently grabbed and caressed her breasts. As she rocked me, my fear faded, replaced by intense pleasure.

They say the eyes are the windows to the soul—and hers, I could not see.

She was blurred at best, but this spirit left me wondering, *why me?* As time passed, the vapor surrounding her began to thin, her features fading in and out. I noticed a vibrant tattoo on her left breast, tongue with a cherry connected by its stem. It was the most beautiful cherry I'd ever seen. Deep red, iridescent, almost alive.

Light pulsed from it as I stared. My mouth watered as if I could taste it—a flavor rich and smooth, like a perfectly aged wine.

She lifted herself to play with her clit. Watching her in my blissful haze, I sat up and sucked her nipple. She continued riding me until, without warning, I felt my orgasm building. I grabbed her waist and bounced her rhythmically. The harder I moved, the louder my heartbeat pounded in my ears.

I squinted, making one last attempt to see her face. Still nothing.

I gave up and closed my eyes, surrendering to the ecstasy. As she rolled her hips, she bent forward and pushed her tongue into my mouth. Her pussy sent powerful sensations racing through my body—so intense my body screamed and shook. It felt like something was being pulled straight through my dick, a pleasure I had never experienced before.

When the sensations finally stopped and I opened my eyes...

She was gone.

Morning crept in as light peeked through the blinds. *Wow... what a night*, I thought. I looked around and noticed my room was exactly as it had been when I laid down—undisturbed. My door was still closed. There was no evidence anything had happened... except for the cum on my thighs and the bed sheets.

My alarm went off at 6:00 a.m. on the dot. I felt an overall calm—the kind that settles in after a night of intense, passionate sex. Damn... she had seemed so real. When I got up, my thighs tingled in the exact places where she had sat.

Unable to rationalize how intense the experience was, I chalked it up to a badass wet dream. *Phew.* And a damn good one at that.

I went to work like nothing had happened. But before the day ended, I caught myself zoning out, replaying View-Master slides of the night before—my encounter with the mystery woman flickering through my mind. Just thinking about busting that nut had me hot and bothered. The last thing I needed was attention drawn to a hard dick at work, so I had to check myself more than once.

There were a couple of moments when I almost lost the battle, the flashbacks of her fucking me too strong to ignore. I had to retreat to a bathroom stall and jack that monkey off my back. There was no way in hell I could tell my boys about this. They'd try to have my ass committed.

Being able to explain last night—and these random sensations—would've been nice... but I decided to leave it alone for now.

Needless to say, every chance I got, I found myself sketching her cherry whenever I had pen and paper. The shit was unreal. I started craving the night before. I couldn't keep my eyes off the clock. I was fucking delirious waiting for quitting time, eager to swipe out because it meant I was that much closer to nightfall.

For someone afraid of ghosts, it tripped me out how anxious I was for her to return.

Maybe this time she'd talk to me while she took me on another journey—*if* it happened. I sat in meetings, questions flooding my mind. Who was she? Where did she come from? Why *me*?

Who am I fooling? I told myself. It was just a wet dream—a vivid one. Or... was it?

Shit was crazy.

I know what, I thought. *I'll videotape myself sleeping—like they do in those paranormal movies.* That way I'd know if I was tripping or not. Maybe I could catch whatever happened while I slept. That had to help.

At least I hoped so.

Night finally fell. It was time to lay it down for the evening. I went through my usual routine, prepping for work the next day. The only difference tonight was setting up the camera to capture anything abnormal while I slept.

I watched TV until my eyelids grew heavy. Ready to turn in, I closed the door, undressed, and climbed into bed. I hoped tonight would bring answers—or at the very least, the same satisfaction as before.

As I drifted off, images of her danced through my mind.

When I opened my eyes, there she stood in the doorway—wearing a chocolate-and-pink polka-dot teddy. This time, the shock was gone. I was excited to see her, curious about what the night would bring.

The glow from the television bounced off the walls, highlighting her figure. Her breasts sat upright, nipples pressing through the fabric. She reached my bed in no time. Her cherry was just as I remembered.

I tried to speak, but she pressed a finger to her full lips.

"Shhh."

A slave to the moment, I obeyed—afraid she might disappear if I didn't. If tonight was anything like last night, I was ready. All five senses were engaged. I was awestruck by her beauty.

The sound of her approaching was soothing. She carried a fragrance that stimulated my taste buds, making me crave the nectar of her being.

When I touched her, her skin felt like silk. I gawked in amazement, licking my lips in anticipation of what was to come.

This time was different. I wasn't paralyzed. I could touch her.

My dick hardened in anticipation of entering her pulsating cavern. She climbed on top of me, positioning herself so I had a full view. What held me captive was the white, cloudy mist floating around her—still hiding her facial features.

She kissed my forehead… my eyelids… my nose… then my lips. Her kisses were soft as cotton and tasted like sweet cherries.

Our kisses were long. Heated.

Without a word between us, she mounted me as she had before. With a solid hard-on, I thought she planned to stay on top. But something strange happened I didn't have to move a muscle. Our bodies levitated, shifting positions simultaneously. Suddenly, she was on the bed, legs spread, and I penetrated her with one smooth motion.

A chill ran up my spine.

I worked hard to make sure she didn't just feel me but received *everything* I had to offer. I arched my back, humping and grinding, filling her with every inch of me. I pushed and pulled—added and subtracted—until she responded, grabbing my back with forceful nails. My skin broke with pleasure as she dug in, transferring some of her energy into me.

My performance reached another level, something almost impossible, some supernatural shit.

I don't know how much time passed, but eventually I was exhausted from the workout. Lost in getting my nut, I didn't even notice when she left.

Again.

Damn.

Discombobulated and pissed at the same time, I checked the clock. It was 9:00 a.m. Light pierced my eyes as I ripped the covers off and looked down at myself. My dick was limp, cum smeared across my thighs—just like I'd finished ejaculating.

With no sign of her presence, I figured it had been another wet dream.

Weak in my knees, I dragged myself to the shower.

Standing at the sink, staring into the bathroom mirror, the longer I looked, the foggier it became. I wiped away the steam when I thought I caught a glimpse of her behind me. I spun around—nothing.

I was tripping.

I shook it off and stepped into the shower. Still feeling horny, I jacked off under the hot water. As the spray pounded my flesh, I turned to let the jets hit my back—and felt a sharp sting.

"What the fuck?"

I jumped out, rushed to the mirror, and froze. Scratch marks—patterns—lined my back.

How could that be?

I shut off the water and hurried back to my room to watch the video. Still dripping, my mind blew apart as I watched myself lying on my back, groping at the air. Sections of the footage blurred with static. I saw myself roll over, grinding like I was fucking the bed.

The mystery was *how* I moved like that.

The static worsened, obscuring everything. Frustrated, I shut the video off. Somehow, seeing it makes things worse. More confusing. Still, I couldn't let it ruin my day, so I got dressed and tried to move on.

Nothing made sense.

All I could remember was her tattoo, the softness of her lips, the faint scent of cherries. Who was she—and why was she haunting me? I found myself studying every woman I encountered, searching for resemblance.

Nothing.

Every night for a week, she returned. And with each visit, she revealed more of herself.

One night, as I drifted off, she appeared again. Feeling bold, I waited until she reached me. Knowing the routine, I stayed silent as she hovered her pussy over my face. She lifted just enough for me to lick her clit.

Her nectar was sweet and satisfying to the palate. Unlike anything I'd ever tasted, and I'd tasted my fair share.

I grabbed her hips, sat up, and flipped her onto her back. Holding her down, I ate her pussy passionately. I searched for some sign that she liked what I was doing—some validation. It felt like I was satisfying myself automatically while satisfying her too.

Our souls were connected.

Sopping up her juices felt like absorbing pieces of her existence, a spirit of pure sensual awakening. Searching for reasons no longer mattered. In my human form, I was overtaken by her sexual power.

When she came in my mouth, I tried to catch every drop as it spilled down my chin. I believed her juices carried something mystical, wasting them felt wrong. I didn't know how long she'd remain, when the dream would end. With each encounter, my desire grew stronger. The thought of her disappearing shook me to my core.

We shifted positions—sixty-nine. I inhaled her scent as I kept eating. Apparently, I wasn't full. In return, she kissed the head of my dick, licking and teasing my balls. She made soft smacking sounds before lifting herself away.

Then she took me in fully.

Up and down, sucking and jacking at the same time. Using every technique, she took my body, my mind, my soul—sending me spinning in a whirlwind of lust. I loved it. I didn't want her to stop.

It didn't take long before pleasure surged through me. My dick spasmed in ways I'd never felt. When I finally came, she sucked like she was drinking through a straw, swallowing every bit of my nut.

It felt like she was feeding.

When she stopped, I was spent.

And once again… she disappeared without warning.

For the next couple of weeks after that wonderful night, she was MIA. I prepared for her each evening like I always did. After the repeated no-shows, I became disenchanted. I had grown obsessed with her, and now I was battling intense anxiety. I couldn't explain why I longed for her so deeply. I started to wonder what the hell was wrong with me.

Without tangible evidence, I finally admitted she was nothing more than a figment of my imagination—yet I had fallen hard for her presence. I knew it wasn't healthy. Before long, I slipped into a mild depression.

Despite my longing, I realized the slump was disrupting my life. Losing her took an emotional toll. I worked hard to keep my days as normal as possible, taking small, gradual steps toward recovery. At first, it didn't seem like a big deal that I hadn't washed my bed linens. I changed the sheets, but not the pillowcases, they where her scent lingered the longest.

Many nights, I found myself cuddled up with that pillow, hugging it and grinding in my sleep, thinking about her. One thing was for sure— two things, actually—it wasn't the same as having her, and I had become sexually frustrated. Eventually, I realized substitutes weren't cutting it, and without any real pussy in my life, the pillowcase routine ended really quick.

After countless nights of sexual frustration, I decided enough was enough. I was fed up—tired of being out of my hookup. I opened my blinds, so to speak. Literally and figuratively, I let the light in. I thumbed through my black book, looking for a real woman to occupy my time.

I'm not a bad-looking guy. Not to sound grandiose, but some even call me "foxy." My six-foot-four muscular frame, 275 pounds, bowed legs—those features had always worked in my favor with women. Within a week, I was back on the circuit… well, sort of.

Like someone obsessed, I'd been focused on one thing, neglecting other important parts of my life. I knew the only way to break the cycle was to get into another relationship. I figured finding something just as attractive and pleasurable might tame the obsession, pull her out of my head, and help me breathe again. I needed balance.

None of my dates measured up. It was a constant battle. Even though I said I was done, I caught myself comparing every woman to her. That was a mistake—because none of them could fuck like she did. I was chasing that same feeling, like a junkie chasing a ghost.

I started wondering if she had been real—someone from my past. If so, I wished I had a name, a number, *something* to find her. Date after date failed, and eventually I decided to lock her away for the sake of my sanity. I needed to move on—find a real woman I could talk to, hold, touch, and feel.

I was fiending.

There were too many nights I went home hard as hell, which over time led to straight-up blue balls. I was tired of jacking myself off. I needed a woman. So, I called Vickii.

She was always good at fulfilling my sexual needs. We'd had great chemistry once. When she said, *this will always be yours*, she meant it. All I had to do was call, and she was Johnny-on-the-spot. The others were… decent.

I remembered how much she loved flowers. Even though this was just a booty call, I could at least show up with a bouquet. I threw on a turtleneck and slacks, nothing flashy. Of course, I added my jewelry: one chain, one ring. I was trying. Things were starting to feel balanced again.

Earlier, I'd had my Beamer truck detailed and filled up. I was ready.

On my way to buy the flowers, driving across East 105th, I noticed a red Mercedes parked at the curb with its hazards blinking. Something told me to stop. A young woman stood behind the car, staring down at a flat tire. Being the gentleman I am, I pulled over.

"Can I help you with that?" I asked, stepping out.

Without a hair out of place, she smiled. "Yeah, I could use a hand— if you don't mind."

As she spoke, I became mesmerized—her eyes, her angelic face. And her body? Banging. What pushed me over the edge was her scent. It was familiar, but I couldn't quite place it. I felt lightheaded, fumbling and stumbling over myself.

"Are you okay?" she asked.

Still dazed, she grabbed my arm, snapping me back. "Yeah—I'm fine. My fault," I said, embarrassed. *Get it together,* I told myself.

"By the way, I'm Chris."

"I'm Charmin. Pleased to meet you, Chris," she said, extending her hand.

The moment I touched her, flashes of my first encounter with the mystery woman rushed back. Charmin was stunning—overwhelmingly so. I felt exposed, vulnerable. There was a strong pull toward her, and I couldn't explain why.

As I changed her tire, images flickered through my mind like a slide projector—click, click—each one carrying emotion and a slight hard-on.

"Well, that should do it," I said, tossing the flat tire into the back of my truck. *Here we go again,* I thought, embarrassed. I closed the trunk slowly, checking to see if my hard-on was noticeable.

"So, Charmin," I asked casually, "where were you headed—if you don't mind me asking?"

"I was on my way to get something to eat," she said.

"Me too—can I join you?" I asked. *Damn*, that just fell out of my mouth. Talk about impulsiveness.

"Sure. I'm heading to Dave's on Lakeshore," she replied. "Have you ever been there?"

"It's been a while," I said, opening her car door for her. "How about I follow you?"

Once back in my truck, I called Vickii to cancel our plans. I promised I'd make it up to her. She was cool with it—we had that kind of relationship.

I followed Charmin to Dave's and parked a few cars away. As I stepped out, I noticed a flower stand down the street from the restaurant. I jogged over, grabbed a bouquet, and caught up to her just as she was getting out of her car.

Things were falling into place.

I handed her the flowers. She smiled, thanked me, and leaned in to smell them. As she reached for the door, I beat her to it, gripping the handle and opening it for her. I wanted to make a good impression.

The place was packed, but we were seated right away.

The waiter approached. "What can I get for you this evening?"

We placed our orders, and he asked if we wanted drinks while we waited.

"What's your best Merlot?" Charmin asked.

"We have Rossi—one of our finest," he replied.

"Give the lady a glass," I said.

The bartender turned to me. "And for you?"

"I'll have the same, please."

He returned shortly with a bottle of Rossi and two wine glasses. Resting the bottle against his arm, he presented the label before opening it. As I glanced down, my breath caught.

The label showed a cherry hanging from its stem, surrounded by a cloudy white mist.

Was I dreaming?

Snap out of it.

As he poured the wine, I looked back at Charmin. "Do you believe in fate?" I asked.

"I do," she said. "Why?"

"I know this might sound corny, but... I've been searching for you."

"Really?" Her eyes locked onto mine—piercing, almost seeing straight through me. "I bet you say that to all the girls."

"Believe it or not, it feels like we've met before. Maybe déjà vu. And please don't think I'm being disrespectful or trying to run game."

She tilted her head. "Go on."

"All right. Don't think I'm crazy, but I dreamt that you came to my bedroom—several nights—and then you just stopped—"

Before I could finish, she smiled, eyes twinkling. She lifted her fingers to her full lips and whispered,

"Shhh... I know."

Chapter Nine

The Consultant

I guess I'm just as freaky as the next bitch. Not to pop my collar, but I might even be freakier than the average hoe. You couldn't tell me I couldn't twerk with the best of them. Fuck it—I could've made a damn video and sold it for $19.99 on an infomercial.

If I had to rate myself back then, I'd give me an A-plus. Confident. Loud. Proud. Holding my own and showing it off. All it took was one open door to show me I wasn't all that. In fact, I got knocked down a peg or two.

Now? I'd say maybe a solid B... C-plus on a bad day. A hard blow to the ego.

So how do I redeem myself?

It took some time to learn a few things, but once I did, it was like hot butter on popcorn. I used to be a flip artist, depending on the mood. Some nights I was conservative. Other nights, I'd fuck the shit out of a nigga like a rabbit in heat—but wouldn't... couldn't... suck a dick.

That little hang-up cost me the love of my life. Taught me a lesson early. So early it made me swear off love altogether.

I don't know if it was a gift or a curse when he left, but I was a whole motherfuckin' hot mess—crying, begging, carrying on. Looking back now, I don't even recognize the bitch staring back at me in the mirror: red-eyed, swollen, nose running, head banging. I was fucked up.

The advice I *should've* given myself. Wipe those fuckin' tears off your face. Throw some cold water on your eyes. Pull up your big-girl panties.

Yeah. Right.

That breakup was a bitter pill to swallow. It took me a minute to dissect and digest what the fuck was really happening. But at some point, I knew I had to get a life. It didn't happen overnight, but when it finally clicked, I was okay.

As the depression lifted, I realized I needed something, *anything,* to occupy my mind. If I didn't, I would've stayed trapped in that dark place, roaming around aimlessly. And if I know anything about myself, it's this: an idle mind is the devil's playground—and I play there really well.

My thoughts kept circling back to him. To the choices I made. To the acts that led to the end of the love life I thought I had locked down.

Some men want their cake—and want to eat it too. That's where the cracks started. The whole scenario replayed in my head like a broken record.

We were together for almost two years. For his birthday, he asked for a ménage à trois.

My first reaction?

HELL. TO. THE. NO.

So, then he asked if someone could just *watch* while we made love.

Let me be clear—I told him I wasn't comfortable with it. I told him it went against my better judgment. But because I loved this man, deeply, I made an exception. Just once.

Now, in my imagination—and maybe with a little wishful thinking— I wondered what would've happened if the ménage had involved another man instead. I doubted he'd be so open to watching another nigga fuck and suck the shit out of me… or two men bumping balls.

Just the thought had me wet.

Maybe there *was* something to this voyeurism shit after all.

But it wasn't about me—it was his birthday. So fuck it. I let him arrange everything. He booked the room, found the spectator, and packed a goody bag.

We met at the DoubleTree on Rockside in Independence. When I heard the knock on the door, my nerves kicked in hard. I had to tell myself to calm down. Once this started, there was no backing out.

She was decent. Nothing special. Nothing to write home about.

But *his* ass?

Ready.

Before I even finished undressing, he was naked, stroking his dick. Since eating pussy was never my thing, the ground rules were laid out beforehand—though I didn't know exactly what *she* had been told.

She went into the bathroom to undress, then took a seat in the corner to watch.

And that's when I saw it.

This idea—this setup—had flipped a switch in him I had never seen before.

That ass was thirsty.

At first, I felt strange allowing her access into our private world. As time passed, I became so wrapped up in him that, for a moment, I forgot she was even there. Since it was his night, I wanted him to have whatever he wished—except oral sex.

He kept insisting that we try something new. Even though I wasn't ready, he didn't hesitate to please me, burying his face between my thighs. The lights in the room were dim; I could barely see her face. What *was* noticeable was her position—sitting in a chair with one leg draped over the arm, pleasuring herself with a dildo. Every so often, I could hear her moaning as she played with her toys and watched us fuck.

He lay on his back in the center of the bed as I straddled his face, on my knees, gripping the headboard. I slid back just enough to squat so his tongue could reach my pussy. In the background, her moans grew louder as he sucked my clit. She seemed to enjoy watching him give me head just as much as I enjoyed receiving it.

He pulled me away from the headboard, letting his legs hang over the bed while he stayed flat on his back. I leaned forward and grabbed a pillow, raising my hips so he could tuck his head beneath me. He cupped my clit with his mouth, licking in slow, deliberate circles. The pressure— his tongue gliding around the base—overwhelmed me. It felt like something was being pulled from my core, but in the best way.

When I looked back, I saw Theresa giving him head, his hips gyrating to her rhythm. As she sucked his dick, he buried his tongue back into my pussy, licking and drinking my juices. I rolled onto my side while he rested his head on the pillow, still working my clit. By then, Theresa had climbed onto the bed, curled in a fetal position with his dick in her mouth. He ground and pumped—side to side, in and out—until his body convulsed. Moaning, he jerked as he came, Theresa jacking his dick as he released into her mouth.

Watching it all was unexpectedly stimulating. Somewhere along the way, I had become a voyeur. It felt good—like we all came together. And I could tell it turned him on, because not long after, he fucked the shit out of me while she watched.

That's when I found out Theresa had started becoming a regular, especially on his paydays. I guess she got tired of not having the whole dick to herself. Or maybe she'd been getting it all along. Either way, she eventually gave him an ultimatum. He took it. And the rest was history.

I still see them sometimes. Our neighborhood is small. And like I said before—I was a fucking wreck.

Eventually, I reorganized my life. I took a few classes and found my niche. During that time, I learned a lot about myself. Some things were positive. Some things were ugly as hell. With that new knowledge, I became a self-proclaimed sexologist—of all things.

Turns out, what one bitch won't do, another will. Careers included.

I maximized my skills and let them work for me. It reminded me of *The Player's Club*: *make the money, don't let it make you.*
Yeah… I watch too much TV.

I got my shit together with the help of my homegirl—my sounding board through it all. I'll always love her for that. Because while my fuck game was spectacular, my refusal to suck dick knocked me down in the ranks. What happened to me was awful. And if I could stop the Theresas of the world from making someone else feel the way I did, then I'd be doing my job.

So, I leveled up.

I became a consultant.

My business focused on men and women struggling to connect sexually with their partners.

They came to me with all kinds of shit.

My services offered both individual and couples' consultations. More often than not, ménage à trois was a recurring topic. I knew my limitations—sometimes clients were referred elsewhere. I had people terrified of losing their partners, some not realizing they'd already lost them. I had clients who were frigid as fuck and didn't even know it. Others were so freaky in bed they couldn't understand why their relationships were failing—the shit they were doing sometimes freaked *me* the fuck out.

It was interesting work.

Not only was I helping people navigate their issues, but I was also learning a thing or two myself along the way. Funny how that works—I was the consultant, yet my clients were teaching me just as much.

I rented office space on the outskirts of town, away from the chaos of the inner city. Given the nature of my business, it was often misconstrued as something shady places of ill repute came with too many regulations and assumptions. My business was legitimate, and I didn't need the extra hassle.

There were no visible signs identifying the services offered. Client privacy was a priority. If you came to see me, it was by referral or invitation only.

In the rear of the office, I had several rooms decorated like a modest three-star hotel—clean, comfortable, and discreet. Nothing fancy, but far from a hole in the wall. Couples checked in for evaluation. Each room was equipped with two-way observation mirrors and video cameras.

It was the client's responsibility to explain the problems they were experiencing. My role was to give them the game—according to my expertise. And when I say *the game*, I mean sexual performance.

Some sessions didn't require me to enter the room. Others did. If instructions were followed and practiced, there was a strong chance the relationship could be saved—or at least improved. That said, we're talking about *possibilities*. Some relationships were already over before they walked through the door.

Because of my own experience with ménage à trois, I approached those cases cautiously. I would assist, when necessary, but something about it always made me uncomfortable. I believed in giving clients a warning before they engaged. If anything, I advised against it. But if they were adamant—well, they proceeded at their own risk.

My first couple was Stephanie and Carlos—old schoolmates. It had been a few years since I'd seen them, which made things a little awkward.

I know what you're thinking, conflict of interest.

In some professions, that would've been an issue. In mine, it wasn't. Enough time had passed, and I knew I could remain professional. Besides, I needed my business to flourish.

Their Case Went Like This

The Assessment

The couple arrived for their scheduled appointment. They were instructed not to bring anything except items that reflected their normal sexual environment—toys, porn, whatever they typically used. They arrived with nothing extra.

Liability paperwork was signed. The room was prepared. They were escorted to their room.

I left and took my position behind the two-way mirror to observe.

As they undressed, he didn't appear particularly excited. She positioned herself on the bed. He climbed on top and began their usual sexual routine.

I took notes.

I watched him kiss her, suck her breasts, rub and caress her body. She remained in a missionary position, passive. She spread her legs. He went down and ate her pussy. He became hard—by my estimation, he was holding close to nine inches. He put in work.

After he busted a nut, she got up and went to shower.

The Meeting

I informed them that during the next session, I would provide instruction while sitting in with them as they had sex. This approach had already been explained during intake. They looked at each other, then agreed.

At the following appointment, I spoke privately with Stephanie—well, that isn't her real name. Real names are never used to protect client confidentiality. She told me she trusted me and was willing to follow my guidance, understanding it was in the best interest of her marriage.

We did a brief ice breaker before proceeding.

They undressed.

As before, he positioned himself between her legs and began sucking her nipples, alternating left to right, kissing her lips in between. I sat in the corner, observing and taking notes.

When he prepared to insert his dick, I quietly stopped them.

Wearing gloves, I instructed them to change positions.

I had him lie on his back and asked her to straddle him. He raised his hips slightly as she lowered herself onto his dick, inch by inch, until she was seated comfortably.

I stepped away.

From there, he took over—pulling her body upward, guiding her down. His facial expression showed clear satisfaction.

Seeing his pleasure, she picked up her pace.

Just as he indicated he was nearing climax, I instructed them to stop and switch positions. I knew this would be difficult, but controlling the sequence was necessary.

I suggested she get on all fours—doggy style—and explained that he would now be entering from behind. I placed his hand on her crotch.

She shivered.

He began fucking her harder and harder.

I told them to give themselves permission to let go.

He started screaming her name, smacking her ass. She chimed in, and soon after, she was close to climax. I dimmed the lights further, exited the room, and allowed them to finish together.

We met several more times before concluding their sessions.

I've had similar encounters with other couples. Some required more foreplay, others needed guidance exploring each other's erotic zones. One tool I found especially helpful was porn—used as education rather than distraction. I kept a library on hand: soft, hard, and everything in between.

The outcomes were consistently successful, especially once couples gave themselves permission to relax, lighten up, and go with the flow.

After consulting for over a year, something shifted.

My business was thriving. My name circulated. I started receiving special attention, discounts from local businesses, free newspapers, flower deliveries. Everything appeared perfect.

Until one day, I had an epiphany.

I missed the companionship of a man.

Working so closely with clients stirred powerful sexual emotions. Watching couples fuck, watching porn stars eat pussy and suck dick—it made me question what was wrong with me.

I realized I had been so invested in other people's sex lives that I'd neglected my own.

Most men I encountered belonged to someone else—and that was a hard no for me. Too much work. Too much mess.

I'd been out of commission for a while and started feeling hypocritical. Here I was advising clients on how to maintain intimacy and save their relationships while I wasn't getting any—and wasn't in one.

My conscience spoke loudly.

I started thinking…Maybe I was the one who needed help.

One day, there was a knock at the door.

It caught me off guard—no one was scheduled for that time. Hesitantly, I opened it.

Standing in front of me was this six-foot-five, dark-complexioned, muscular giant of a man. His eyes were captivating, dimples cut deep into his cheeks. For a split second, I swear I saw a beam of light shining down from the sky, hovering right over his head. Fine—he was absolute eye candy. I was impressed.

Being celibate, spending my days watching and assisting couples with their sex lives, my imagination immediately went into overdrive. Funny thing was, I hadn't really cared much about what I was missing… until this heavenly creation fell right onto my doorstep.

"Hello, my name is Javez," he said. "I just moved into the apartment building across the street. I've noticed you coming and going since I got here. The other day, when it was raining, I wanted to come help you—it looked like you were struggling with your packages. But before I could make it downstairs, you managed to get inside. Sorry."

So… he'd been watching me.

Oh, how original, I thought.

"Well, that was very thoughtful," I replied. "I appreciate it." I glanced at the clock. "Listen, I'm sorry, but I have an appointment in about ten minutes, so I—"

"Oh, I understand," Javez said quickly. "I'll let you go. But before I do—what's your name?"

"My name is Ebony," I answered. "Ebony Lezyah."

"Well, Ebony," he said with a smile, "would it be okay if I called you? Maybe invite you to lunch—not today, but tomorrow? Supposed to be nice weather. Sun shining… you know, a typical Cleveland day."

"Well, I usually don't…" I said, hesitant.

"Come on," he pressed lightly. "We can meet at the restaurant down the street. It's on me."

I paused. "Okay. How about 1:30?"

"Perfect. I'll see you tomorrow."

As he turned to leave, he added, "It was really nice meeting you."

When I closed the door, I stood there for a moment, stunned.

What the *fuck* was that?

I couldn't believe this man had just appeared at my door like he dropped straight out of the sky.

Mmm… Javez.

I guess it's a date.

After lunch, Javez asked me out again. He seemed like a genuinely nice guy, so I accepted. One date turned into several. Weeks have passed. Then months.

I couldn't believe half a year had gone by so quickly. Time really does fly when you're having fun. I found myself genuinely liking him, something I hadn't planned on at all after my breakup.

I blamed it on leftover PTSD from my last relationship. Still healing. Still cautious. Okay… maybe not *that* serious—but it had been devastating at the time.

We spent a lot of time together. Things felt so good that I started wondering how long it could last. Pinch me—wake me up. He felt too good to be true.

Eventually, I told him what I did for a living.

He found it fascinating.

Intrigued, even.

That opened the door to deeper conversations. He listened. Asked questions. Made me feel seen. Special.

That's when I had to sit with myself—really sit with myself—and do some soul searching.

If I could help others make it happen in their relationships… maybe it was time to make it happen for myself.

Satisfaction wasn't the problem.

I even started taking my own advice—giving myself permission to let go.

Maybe even… sucking a little dick along the way.

The day finally came.

I decided to let my guard down and officially retire my celibacy. I went to his apartment for dinner and an evening of relaxation. I was a little anxious—which was funny, considering I was the sex consultant.

His place wasn't just an apartment.

It was a penthouse, complete with a panoramic view of the city. The furnishings were the finest money could buy—clean lines, rich textures, intentional luxury. I remembered him mentioning that he was an analyst, but I had been so wrapped up in talking about my own business that I never pressed for details. Now, seeing his space, I wished I had.

His office alone was massive and plush. Not only did he have multiple computers, but several servers lined the walls.

As he prepared dinner, he casually explained, "I work as a high-end broker."

I paused. *What the hell is that?*

"I own my company," he continued, "with a team of international researchers who study market trends. We consult investors on when to buy and sell."

"That's… impressive," I said honestly.

Javez was far more accomplished than I initially realized.

"Well," he said with a smile, "enough about me. Let's eat."

My plate was full—T-bone steak, macaroni and cheese, spinach, sweet cornbread. For dessert, apple pie. The meal was thoughtful, comforting, and delicious.

Afterward, we sat out on his patio, sipping wine and enjoying the night air.

"What an evening," he said. "Are you sleeping over tonight?"

"I hadn't planned on it," I replied.

"I like you," he said calmly. "And I want to be with you. This isn't business, it's personal. Do you understand what I'm saying?"

"I do," I said. "You're not one of my clients."

"Come with me," he said.

We went into his bedroom. The ambiance was breathtaking—the city lights stretched endlessly beyond the balcony windows. As I stood taking it all in, he returned with a bottle of wine and two glasses.

He sat on the bed and picked up a remote. The lights dimmed, leaving a soft glow in the center of the room. With another click, a ring of ceiling lights illuminated around us. Then the room darkened again—and the ceiling transformed.

Stars.

An entire star map stretched above us. He pointed out constellations—some familiar, others completely new to me. The surround sound system filled the room with music so crisp it felt like the musicians were performing live.

It was surreal.

"The bathrooms through that door," he said, handing me a robe. "Freshen up if you'd like. Make yourself at home."

In the bathroom, I undressed and turned on the shower, letting the steam fill the space. I stood in front of the mirror, studying myself—really looking. When the glass fogged over, I wiped it clean and stared back again, thinking about what I was about to do.

Fuck it.

I grabbed a washcloth and stepped into the shower.

The master bath was stunning, a walk-in combination shower and sauna, complete with body sprayers. Water fell from above like warm rain, ambient lights glowing softly. I sat on the built-in bench, letting the music and water wash over me, losing track of time entirely.

When I finished, it was his turn to shower. I returned to the balcony, gazing at the skyline once more.

He emerged naked, towel draped casually as he dried his hair.

"Another glass of wine?" he asked.

"Just a little," I said.

He raised his glass. "A toast—to us. May our relationship blossom."

"To us," I replied.

Our glasses touched. He leaned in, and we shared a long, unhurried kiss.

He lay back on the bed, inviting me to join him. I could already feel his presence, his confidence, his patience. He understood foreplay, but more than that, he knew how to stimulate the mind.

Before anything physical happened, anticipation alone had me fully engaged. Between the music, the atmosphere, and his touch, I was already there.

He gently parted my legs, lowering himself slowly until he was face to face with my center.

"Bonjour, mademoiselle," he murmured. "Comment allez-vous ce soir?"

"Amende… et vous?" I replied.

I guess Mrs. Kirby's French class at John Hay finally paid off.

French was such a romantic language. I'd always imagined what it would feel like—having a man speak it to me in moments like this.

Mystical. Intimate. And undeniably sexy. He had already taken me to another level.

He looked up and smiled as he continued to seduce me with soft French niceties. He licked me slowly, then blew gently, sending chills rippling through my body.

It didn't stop there.

"Es bueno para tú, bebé," he murmured as he sucked my clit. Then he translated softly, "Is that good for you, baby?" His tongue circled with intention, precise and controlled.

He slipped two fingers inside me, massaging in slow, deliberate circles while continuing to suck my clit. She was swollen, sensitive. Whatever maneuver he performed next triggered a chain reaction I couldn't stop.

"Tayari... tayari," he repeated.

Swahili: ready?

Each time he whispered *tayari*, he increased his speed. The sensation intensified, building rapidly.

It was like the Domino Effect—waves of pleasure colliding and spreading throughout my body. The contractions traveled from my clit, through my vagina, and up into my pelvis. The sensation built and built until—

I climaxed.

Phew.

He kissed me from head to toe—and figuratively, my mind. I never expected his tongue to expose me to such an expansive world of ecstasy. Some of the languages he spoke were unfamiliar, yet he brought them to life. Even when he explained their meaning, my body acted as the interpreter.

He took me on a world tour—places I never imagined I'd go.

It was deeply romantic.

Any inhibitions I'd carried into the evening dissolved. I was so consumed by him that I was ready to reciprocate—to expand *his* world now. It was my turn to shift positions. I didn't need introductions or foreign phrases. What I was about to give him was universal.

I went for it.

As he lay there, watching me, I kissed him slowly, deliberately. His fingers slid into my hair as I focused my attention on him. He began to move with me, guiding my rhythm. I followed instinctively confident, present, intentional.

Every muscle in his body tense.

"Damn, baby," he breathed.

I guess I learned a thing or two from observation after all.

Just as he reached his peak, he pulled me back and finished himself, watching me as he did. Afterward, he pulled me into him, kissing me deeply.

As we lay together, Javez told me the evening brought meaning into his life. He said he'd been with women all over the world, but there was something about me—something different. I was flattered. Hearing that the experience was just as powerful for him stirred something deep inside me.

As he spoke, I could feel him responding again. His words, his touch all worked together. He had a way of drawing me into submission, but gently, consensually, beautifully.

And I wanted to follow wherever he led.

Listening to him share such intimate thoughts lifted me—emotionally and physically. My mind and body opened to the possibilities of what this connection could become. I hadn't felt this way in a long time.

I felt light. Whole. Secure.

Another chapter in my life was opening.

Stepping outside my comfort zone had been risky—but right now, at this moment, I was suspended in bliss.

As Javez opened himself to me, I found the courage to do the same. It wasn't easy. You'd think someone who talks for a living would find it simple—but parts of my life have always been guarded. Making love to him helped tear down some of those walls.

Lying in his arms, learning him, being learned by him—it taught me more than I expected.

We lay there afterward, music playing softly, stars glowing across the ceiling. It was clear this was more than lust. There was real bonding happening.

When he moved again, slowly and intentionally, I responded instinctively. My body welcomed him, already warmed by his words and touch.

"Ahhhh," I moaned as he moved, steady and controlled, speaking softly in languages I didn't recognize but somehow understood.

Our bodies found a rhythm—natural, synchronized. When he whispered to me, I felt transformed. Present. Renewed.

I murmured, "This your pussy."

He paused. Smiled.

"This is my pussy?" he repeated. "Let me show you."

What followed felt inevitable—our connection deepening, bodies responding in perfect alignment. When we reached that peak together, it wasn't just release—it was confirmation.

Every muscle tightened. Energy surged. The release traveled through me completely.

That— was a full-body orgasm.

Javez leaned back in his chair, wiping the sweat from his forehead. He pulled his chair closer to mine and kissed me softly.

"Tell you what," he said. "I have a business trip coming up next month in the Bahamas. Come with me. I'll take care of everything—you won't have to worry about a thing."

"Well?" I said, raising an eyebrow.

"Before you say no," he continued, smiling, "I want you to think about it… and give me your answer in ten minutes." He laughed. "No, no—I'm kidding. If you need time, I understand. I just want to make reservations."

He paused, then added, "I own a little piece of property near the ocean. You'll love it. You've got to come with me. This is something I want to share with you. You'll have time to make arrangements with your business. Come on—go with me. I'll make it worth your while."

"I don't know what to say," I admitted.

"Say yes," he said simply. "We'll tour the island, eat amazing food, drink good wine, and make love by the ocean—all expenses paid. Don't worry. I've got you. Say yes."

"Yes," I said, laughing. "Wow. An all-expense-paid trip, what was there to think about? I'll have to work on that."

"Come on," he said, reaching for the bottle. "Let's toast. Where's your glass?" He poured the wine and raised his. "To love—and to our future."

As I sipped, he looked at me and said, "I can show you better than I can tell."

We finished the bottle on the patio, laughing and talking. I felt good satisfied in a way that went beyond the physical. I didn't know if what I was feeling was infatuation or love, but it felt right.

I'm going to the Bahamas, I'm going to the Bahamas, I sang quietly to myself.

Love is a funny thing.

When my world was rocked, I was devastated. I reached out to others just to keep my head above water. At times, I escaped into denial—giving advice, giving "the game," even while something was missing in my own life.

Some people never experience love—not even from their parents. Love comes in many forms, from many places. People search for it, or what they believe love should be, sometimes in all the wrong spaces. One day they love someone with everything they have, and the next day that love is gone. So, they keep trying—loving, pleasing, hoping—when sometimes, it just doesn't work.

People fall out of love.

Love doesn't always come easy. But when you find it, when it's genuine and unconditional, it's a blessing.

For a long time, I believed that performing well in bed was enough. Sex is one thing—but love is another. I shared my understanding of sexual fulfillment with many, yet something was missing from those lessons—including my own life.

Once I realized that absence, I was eventually blessed to love again. I didn't immediately understand how that love had been disrupted or stolen, and I stayed in denial longer than I should have, perhaps living through my clients instead of myself.

But it was up to me not to stay down.

I got up.

What I finally found was what had been missing all along loving myself, and finding someone who loved me for who I truly am.

Chapter Ten

Eight Chapters

I felt uneasy and knew damn well I shouldn't have wagered a bet against Sandy. I never win. I think she knew I was going to lose—shit, I *knew* I was going to lose. But I had to be grown and gamble in a no-win situation anyway.

She had this sick, twisted plan to get me to disclose the intricate details of my love life. And she won. To make sure I kept it honest, she made me swear to tell the whole truth and nothing but the truth—so help me.

Thursday night, I laid my cards on the table.

She chose her support group, *Eight Chapters*, for me to air my dirty laundry in front of her and a bunch of strangers. I had no choice. A bet is a bet.

Damn.

The room, with its yellow-stained walls, was thick with the smell of stale cigarette smoke and the low hum of people talking—broken up by the occasional cough. Smoke rings floated lazily in the air, disappearing as they reached the flickering fluorescent lights. You could tell the room had seen years of use; even the bulbs themselves were tinted with smoke stains.

About twenty-five chairs were arranged in five rows, all facing a podium with a microphone. Most of the people seated looked like everyday folks, but a few characters gave off a slightly shady vibe. Hell, for all I knew, they were probably thinking the same thing about me.

Either way, we were all there for the same reason, support. To talk about our addictions. To share our feelings.

The facilitator was about to wrap up the meeting and asked if anyone else wanted to share. Sandy raised her hand, announcing that she'd brought a newcomer who was interested in speaking.

In that instant, my breath grew heavy. I felt light-headed, my palms were damp. The group responded with warm applause. I stood and walked toward the podium, I felt a wave of nausea roll through me. It was like the room expanded with every step as if I were walking the green mile.

After listening to everyone else's stories, I wondered what the hell I could even say. I took a deep breath and began.

"I don't know if it was the sex or the pleasure of being wanted. He had a darkness about him, an allure that called to me, he pulled me in. An undeniable swag. I could have had many, but for some reason I kept returning to the memory of what he gave me. Eight chapters as therapy for my soul. To remind myself that I was addicted to a mirage.

I paused.

"My name is Charmin," I said. "And this is my story."

"Hi, Charmin," the group replied in unison.

Chapter One – The Meeting

It's funny how you can go to the same place repeatedly and never cross paths with everyone who frequents it. Timing is everything.

As I pulled into the store's parking lot, a small group stood nearby talking. They moved to the side as I parked. The noise hit me immediately when I stepped out of my car. Surveying the crowd, my eyes locked onto this fine, short, thick, chocolate *brutha*.

Damn—he was fine.

His eyelids sat low, and I couldn't tell if it was from whatever he'd been into or if they were just naturally dreamy. I walked past him like I didn't notice a thing, using the hell out of my peripheral vision until he was out of sight.

Hopefully, he'll still be here when I come back.

When I returned to my car after leaving the store, my eyes zoomed right back in on him. He caught me completely off guard when he grabbed my hand. I wasn't expecting that at all—and what was crazy was that I *had* been watching him, yet I still didn't see it coming.

Startled, my instinct was to pull away. You'd think he would've known better than touch someone he didn't know like that was inappropriate. When he realized how I reacted, he apologized, then immediately tried to introduce himself.

I spoke briefly and kept walking toward my car. He followed, continuing to apologize for approaching me the way he did. As I opened my door, he asked my name. I told him, and we made a little small talk. Before I knew it, we'd exchanged phone numbers.

Then I left.

As I continued on my way, I questioned whether that was the right thing to do.

Oh well…

Chapter Two – The First Encounter

A few hours later, I finally made it home from couponing. I did really well that day, but I was exhausted after all those successful hauls. All I wanted was to relax. Images of my bed dancing in my head, and I knew the moment my head hit the pillow, I'd be out cold.

And that's exactly what happened.

Hours later, my phone rang, jolting me awake. Checking the caller ID, I saw an unfamiliar number. *Damn.* It was two o'clock in the morning—who the hell was calling at this hour?

I answered, slightly irritated.

"Hello?"

I couldn't quite make out what the person was saying, so I asked, "Who is this?"

A deep, sensual voice called my name. "Charmin?"

It sounded like a question—like he wasn't sure he had the right person. Once I shook off the grogginess, recognition hit.

It was him.

I sat up, cleared my throat, and answered, "Yes, this is she… Khalid?"

"Yes," he said. "How are you? I hope you don't mind me calling. I was just lying here thinking about you."

"Well, no—it's okay," I replied. "How are you?"

"Better now that I hear your voice."

I couldn't help but smile. He was smoothly spitting mad game. And I was receptive to it. I've been known to have a little game myself.

Since it was the weekend, I didn't rush to get off the phone. We talked for hours. Here he was, a complete stranger, and yet we covered so much laughing about people he knew, stories about his family. By the time we hung up, I felt like I'd learned a lot about him.

What surprised me most was how much we had in common.

As days passed, our conversations grew deeper and more frequent. I shared some of my most intimate moments, and he listened—really listened. I felt comfortable talking about anything and everything. Months went by, and I believed our connection had reached another level.

Looking back, I realize that was part of his game.

Unfortunately, I didn't know I was playing.

So, imagine my surprise when I found out…he already had a woman.

Chapter Three – The Hook, Line, and Sinker

Even though we spent days and nights in each other's company, there still wasn't a strong commitment between us. Sure, he'd introduced me to some of his friends and family, but things hadn't gelled to the point where we were an actual couple. About two months in, we decided it was time to take things to the next level.

Sex was the common factor.

I mean *sex*—though I'm sure emotions played a role, to some degree. I felt comfortable with him and was curious to see what it would be like to fuck him.

So, we planned a rendezvous to get to know each other in a more intimate way. We met at the Econo Lodge, about twenty minutes off the E-way. My overnight bag was packed—lingerie, condoms, and sex toys, just in case he was a lazy fuck or liked to play. Either way was fine with me. I planned to bust at least one.

The room wasn't fancy, but it worked for our purpose—two beds, a bathroom, and a TV. Pumped, I stepped inside, dropped my bag by the door, and paused, plotting my next move. I was anxious to see what he was working with. He talked a good game—now it was time to put up or shut up.

I undressed him with my eyes until I was hot from anticipation, like I'd created my own personal summer.

I wasn't worried about my end of things. I was confident in my skills. He stripped down and—*booyah*. Long, thick, fat-ass dick. Damn. Half the battle was already won. Proof was in the pudding… but could he work that motherfucka'? It's sad when a nigga has a fat-ass dick and doesn't know what to do with it.

He stood naked at the foot of the bed, dick in hand, the glow from the TV outlining his body.

I could tell he was just as ready as I was.

That's when Nah Nah started talking to me. Yeah—Nah Nah. Men name their dicks all the time—Johnston, Fred, Dickey—so it's only right

I name my pussy. She got her name from Foxy Brown's *Ill Na Na* because she's a bad bitch, and I knew my shit was bad.

Nah Nah has a mind of her own. When she pulsates and flinches, I listen. Talking hot, I have absolutely no say-so.

Lying back in missionary, legs wide open, I introduced him to Nah Nah. She jumped to life as he stroked himself. He crawled between my legs and entered her world of ecstasy. As he ate me out, Nah Nah quivered like a 9.0 on the Richter scale.

His tongue had a conversation with her.

He went from stroking her lips to teasing her clit. Her muscles twitched. I shivered, overwhelmed by the pleasure of his touch. Wanting more, I spread my legs wider, giving him full access. He kissed her from head to split, sometimes holding my legs while rocking my body side to side as he licked and sucked.

He worked her clit—up and down, side to side, round and round—until I was climbing the bed, trying to escape my own body.

The intensity built fast. I grabbed his head, holding him in place while I rolled my hips. With every movement, my moans grew louder. His tongue covered every inch of her. I felt his fingers slide inside, moving in and out, side to side, hitting my G like a vibrator.

I thought about pulling out my Pink Wave vibrator—had even packed it to see if he'd play—but he didn't need it. He had me speaking in tongues.

Nah Nah started twitching.

As I got close, I screamed his name between the *oohs* and *ahhs*. I closed my eyes, breathing heavily, forcing his head down as he worked faster and harder. My body shook as the wave hit. Once Nah Nah reached the point of no return, everything else shut down.

She was the puppet master—pulling every string in my body.

Climax rippled through me like waves after a pebble hits water. My body rode it until my pussy pulsed. Yeah—she needed a little head and a little dick along the way, but Nah Nah? She's a bad bitch.

Damn.

That orgasm was everything.

He crawled up, dreamy-eyed, ready to penetrate. He rubbed his dick along her, searching for his way in. Nah Nah wanted more but needed a second to recover. The clit doesn't stay asleep long—just hit the right spot.

I guided him in. He teased, pressing just the tip, grinding like he was performing a ritual. In and out, lifting his body, moving slowly. Nah Nah woke right back up.

He plunged forward and deep.

Our bodies locked together, moving in rhythm, lost to everything else. It was just us. The man had stamina—straight longevity. Luckily, I stayed wet, or I would've been on fire from the friction.

He talked nasty, telling me to cum. And yeah—this motherfucka was *bad*. I called on Nah Nah to take over.

She did.

She flexed, pulled, pushed—rocking his world. He screamed as she squeezed him dry. He came hard. So did I.

The shit was good as fuck.

He rolled onto his back, spent.

Nah Nah had done her job.

She did it…and he liked it.

Chapter Four – The Compromise

Our first night together was the bomb. I think I was dick matized. Every time I thought about him, Nah Nah's waterfall started flowing. So needless to say, whenever he wanted to fuck, I was game.

After that night, most of our sexual encounters mirrored the first. I shared every detail with Bleu—my bestie. I couldn't wait to tell him about Khalid's fuck game and how this nigga had me completely whipped.

Excited, Bleu's first response was, "You never said anything about sucking his dick."

"I'm not into that… like that," I said, looking at him crazy.

"If you want to keep this man happy, you're gonna have to suck *something*," he replied. "He's eating you, right? So, lesson one in satisfying a man—put the dick in your mouth."

He broke it down from a man's perspective—what parts of a dick needed the most attention, how to have a nigga calling out your name. He called it educating me. School was in session, and Ms. Claudia Rodriguez was teaching.

After talking it through, I realized he was right about a few things. I made up my mind that the next time Khalid and I met, I'd be playing for keeps. If it meant putting his dick in my mouth, then that's exactly what I'd do.

I practiced a little—with a Popsicle. Cherry, to be exact.

We grew more adventurous. Instead of traveling far to get rooms, we started fucking in nearby hotels and motels. Rarely did we spend the night—we met to fuck and then kept it moving. If we wanted to hang out, that could happen another time. For us, sex was serious business.

We met at one motel that was an upgrade from the usual sleazy holes-in-the-wall. With no time to waste, I treated him like a Nubian king.

I ran his bathwater naked while he watched me flaunt my ass, keeping the momentum going. As I tested the water, I felt him behind me. I never imagined his dick would find its way to my ass like that. Semi-limp, he invited himself into a quick exploration.

He slid in from behind, fucking me as I braced myself on the edge of the tub while it filled. My arms weakened under pressure, and I nearly slipped—saved only by the grab bar. After he busted his first nut, he climbed into the tub, where I washed him... and his royal penis.

After drying him off, we moved to the bed—where I planned to show him everything I'd learned.

I kissed him slowly, from his lips to his hips. I sucked, flicked, and rolled my tongue over his nipples, glancing up occasionally to watch his reactions. There's something about seeing a man aroused that turns me on even more.

My kisses traveled from the center of his chest, down his abs, circling his belly button—setting the stage for a brand-new experience.

His breathing grew heavy as he grabbed and wrinkled the sheets. Nah Nah began to pulsate.

I continued downward, licking the rim of his head. His legs stiffened, toes pointing as he rocked his hips, guiding my tongue. Letting go of the sheets, he grabbed my hair, pulling it into a ponytail.

I kissed and sucked his balls, one at a time, massaging them with my tongue. Pulling back, I traced figure eights along his shaft, speeding up and slowing down. He moaned loudly, tightening his grip.

He guided my head to his tip. I stretched my tongue and licked from the base to the crown. His dick jumped—I knew he was enjoying it.

Feeling playful, I looked up and asked what he'd named his dick.

"Shaft," he said.

I nearly laughed. That was the weirdest name I'd heard yet. I kept my composure, chuckling quietly, then took him back into my mouth—spiraling my tongue around the crown. I added and subtracted inches, controlling the depth so I wouldn't gag. Pulling away, I jacked him at alternating speeds.

I wanted to feel his release.

Moments later, cum filled my mouth. I reached for a towel and spit.

Then I laid back, legs open. It was time for Shaft and Nah Nah to do what they did best. Rolling onto my back, I welcomed him. Nah Nah almost seemed to sigh in relief.

He went to work—fucking the shit out of me.

We started with me on my back. By the time we finished, I was face down, ass up, my back marked with sucker bites. Gasping, he collapsed beside me. I curled into his arms for a quick kiss.

The rendezvous satisfied us both.

We showered together, sharing a little afterplay before getting dressed. Afterward, we embraced, got into our cars, and went our separate ways.

As time went on, he grew lax—like the honeymoon was over. That's when I learned the truth: I wasn't the only woman in his life. Worse, he was actually living with her.

I know what you're thinking, how didn't I know? We met at hotels. But I initiated that setup. I didn't want him at my place either. I was blinded by the dick. I ignored signs, excused red flags, stayed in denial.

Out of sight, out of mind.

I wanted him badly enough to overlook that little detail. All I cared about was that when it was my turn, he licked, sucked, and fucked the shit out of Nah Nah.

And the shit was good.

We fucked more often—anytime, anywhere. Outside. Parking lots. By the lake. My house. Someone else's house. His apartment. No place was off-limits. We'd cruise around, find dark spots, and hit the back seat.

Back seats aren't as small as people think.

Hell, it got to the point where a finger fuck would do.

Crazy, right?

Chapter Five – Jealousy

After three months of nonstop fucking and sucking, I met someone else. He was tall, dark, and handsome. His name was Chris—nothing serious yet. Khalid didn't take too kindly to our sessions dwindling. I wasn't always available when he called.

His jealousy was obvious the first time he saw Chris and me together.

On nights when Khalid and I were out, no one could show me attention without him catching an attitude. At first, I thought the shit was cute—until he got into a fight with one of his homeboys for touching my ass. It wasn't even that serious. The man had brushed against me trying to get past in a crowded party.

I had to talk to Khalid about his anger. He was getting out of control.

What I couldn't understand was why he was so upset. I'd played his game without tripping. And if he couldn't handle it, I was prepared to let his ass go. Then he had the nerve to say *I* was taking *him* on an emotional and sexual roller coaster.

So, he gave me an ultimatum.

Ain't that a bitch?

He told me if I didn't end things with my new boo, he wouldn't fuck me anymore. That was cold—and fucked up. Now I really felt like a piece of ass, taken for granted. To keep the peace, I told him I'd think about it.

Besides, I wanted to see if Nah Nah approved of Chris's fuck game.

I know—I should've cared about more than sex. But sex is a major part of who I am and how I tick. I thought Chris might help me wean myself off Khalid.

I enjoyed my time with Chris, and my time with Khalid faded. Khalid caught an attitude and decided to cut me off. I guess that made it official.

If I'm being honest, Chris had a nasty fuck game too. He was no joke. Still, thoughts of Khalid kept resurfacing. There was something about him that made Nah Nah long for him.

Chapter Six – Grudge Fuck

Six months have passed after our so-called breakup. I hadn't seen or heard from Khalid once. Early on, he blocked my number and stopped showing up at his usual spots. It was like he disappeared.

Then his cousin invited me to her birthday party—and you already know I went. I figured Khalid would be there with his new boo, so I left Chris at home. That gave me room to move.

Butterflies fill my stomach. I kept thinking about what could go wrong after all that time.

The party was lit. I met a lot of new people—and just like I expected, Khalid was there. Even with another woman on his arm, he kept mean-mugging me like I'd done him wrong.

Nah Nah wasn't laughing.

We had history, and I still had feelings for him. He stirred something in her. She started moving to her own rhythm. I tried to channel her down, but she took over—like the puppet master she is.

Before the night was over, I was standing right in front of him.

We talked. I won't lie—I kept glancing at his dick. Don't judge me. Women do it. Men stare at breasts all the time. By the imprint in his pants, I could tell Shaft missed Nah Nah as much as she missed him.

I went to the hotel desk and booked a room, not knowing if he'd even show. Back at the party, I slipped a key card on him and told him to meet me in Suite 104.

He didn't decline.

After mingling a bit longer, I went upstairs. When I opened the door, he was already in bed, stroking himself. I started stripping immediately. He hovered over me, spread my legs, and shoved his finger inside.

"What the fuck?" I spoke. "That was rough."

"Shut up and get ready to take this dick," he snapped.

I tried to push him away. He covered my mouth and forced my legs apart, slamming Shaft into Nah Nah. I wasn't ready. It wasn't the same. He wasn't the same.

He fucked with vengeance.

He whispered about how pissed he was seeing me with another man. I struggled at first, then went still detached. He didn't care if I was involved. He just wanted to get off.

No foreplay. No care. Just straight to it.

I cried. Nah Nah eventually relaxed, there was no other option. The dick was still stimulating, and part of me responded, but my mind refused to give him that satisfaction. He acted like he was proving I was addicted to his sex.

When he said, *"We doing grown folks' shit, so act like it and take that dick,"* something snapped.

Fuck him.

I wrapped my legs around him, flipped him over, and climbed on top. Now *I* was in control. I rode him hard, bit his nipples, gave him some of that pain back. We fucked for over an hour. I came harder than I had in a long time—crying from desire and anger.

He begged me to squeeze him while I rode until he busted.

Afterward, he yelled about how angry he got seeing me with another man.

"Whatever," I said. "We wouldn't be here if you hadn't lied to me."

He grabbed my arm when I tried to leave. I pulled away and walked out.

That's when I knew—it was over.

This nigga was crazy as fuck.

And I was done.

Chapter Seven – The Departure

I had to be strong and move on. I couldn't let him continue to dominate my sexual thoughts and fantasies. He was a drug, and I was addicted to his love. There were times when he called and I went running—literally. I had been compromising myself.

I thought about him often, and Nah Nah wanted to welcome Shaft back within her walls. I knew this was a recipe for disaster—one I had to fight. What was once good for me was no longer an option. I had to close these chapters of my life. Someone once told me that all dick isn't good dick, even when it *is* good dick.

I continued my relationship with Chris, spending as much time with him as possible. It helped that I genuinely enjoyed his company and that being with him felt healthy. I was developing real feelings for him, and that helped pull my focus away from Khalid.

An idle mind is the devil's playground. Whenever I had too much time alone, my thoughts drifted right back to Khalid. That's when I realized how important it was for me to have someone who could help pick up the pieces.

And I found that in Chris.

We talked openly about our past relationships. It took me a while to let my guard down. He didn't know about that night with Khalid at the hotel—and he didn't need to. What mattered was that he understood healing is a process. He gave me space to let go in my own time.

That's what made him special.

He fulfilled my days—and my nights.

Chapter Eight – The Reminiscence

Now that I've broken his spell—at least I think I have—I don't crumble when our paths cross. Unfortunately, we still frequent some of the same places. When he sees me, I can see the lust in his eyes. There were many nights we fucked and sucked, rode hard and took doggie style like champs. He enjoyed it as much as I did, there's no denying that.

What I went through was enough to teach me a lifetime's worth about men like Khalid. And with that knowledge, I've made peace.

Did I compromise myself for nights of pleasure? Absolutely. It was a hard habit to break. There were times the phone rang, and I hoped it was him. I used to run at his beck and call. Even now, there are moments when seeing him brings a flicker of pain.

At one point, it was so bad I'd see someone in a crowd and think it was him. My body went through real withdrawal—like an addict detoxing. I had to work hard to confront those feelings. I kept reminding myself that I was happy with what I had.

I was haunted—but I was dealing with it.

That's why I stand before you now, asking for help. I need to close these chapters of my life. I'm addicted to sex with a man who is not good for me—a man who hijacked my mind. My body craves him like a drug.

So… that's my story.

My name is Charmin,

and I am an addict.

"Thank you, Charmin, for sharing," the facilitator said. "This is the first step to recovery—admitting you have a problem."

7:30 p.m. — St. Aloysius High School Gymnasium - Eight Chapters, Southside

"This is new for me. I'm usually the listener," he said. "But after hearing some of your stories, I think it's time I share mine."

"That's all right—take your time," someone called out.

"Okay… here goes. I don't know if it was love or just one of my many flings. When she stepped out of her car, she glowed. She was like a burst of sunshine breaking through the clouds on a rainy day. I know that sounds corny, but you had to be there—to see her through my eyes—to understand.

"Her presence demanded attention. When our eyes met, I felt a connection, like I was chosen. The way she walked showed confidence—that she knew who she was, that she was intelligent and strong. She was a beautiful woman with undeniable swag, and that's exactly what I needed."

He paused, then continued.

"After getting to know her mind, body, and soul, I knew she was a keeper. But by then, I was set in my ways. You know how hard it is to break bad habits. I was greedy. I had a woman—hell, I had many women. I couldn't commit to her, and because of that, I lost her.

"I even had the nerve to get angry when she started dating. I should've left well enough alone. Because of me—because of my ego—we're no longer together. All I have now are memories. If I had been as accepting as she was, we'd still be together."

He took a breath.

"So, I'm here to share my story—to remind myself that I'm addicted to the one I let get away. My name is Khalid, and this is how it all started. Let me tell you my story."

"Hi, Khalid," the group responded together.

"Our eyes connected when she walked past. She tried to play hard and ignored me. I refused to let her get away, so when she came back, I grabbed her hand. When she pulled away, the warmth she left behind hit me, and my heart dropped. I knew I had to talk to her.

"When the opportunity came, I jumped in headfirst.

"One thing about her—she was a talker, and I loved to listen. Whatever weighed on her, my ears were open. Her intellect kept me on my toes. I learned a lot from her. The time we spent together was unlike anything else.

"But I was a slave to my greed. I wanted my cake and to eat it too. Things were going well until I let my guard down and she found out about the others. She accepted it—as long as I handled my business. Over time, she jumped rank and became my main line. The others were just that—others.

"I fucked it up when I let my emotions take over. I became jealous.

"The sex… the sex was mind-blowing. I think about her even when I'm with someone else. Nah Nah—she was indescribable. And yeah, Nah Nah is a big part of why I'm here."

He shook his head slightly.

"It feels strange standing here today. This isn't how I usually move. Somewhere between having my cake and eating it too, I fell in love—at least, that's what I call it now. I just didn't know it then.

"I'm addicted to sex. I'm addicted to love. And I'm addicted to Charmin."

On the Other Side of Town

A different meeting. Same time.

"My name is Khail," he said.

And his story echoed hers.

He loved her. Lost her. Greed had cost him everything.

"I'm addicted to sex. I'm addicted to love. I'm addicted to Charmin."

About the Author

Hayzel Greene is a native Clevelander who currently resides in the Glenville community on the northeast side of Cleveland, Ohio. She attended Cleveland Public Schools as a Major Works and Honor student and later went on to earn her master's degree in business.

As an only child, Hayzel often entertained herself in ways that nurtured her imagination and intellectual curiosity. Reading, writing, and playing electronic games were favorite pastimes. Like many little girls, she also spent countless hours playing with doll-creating characters, worlds, and storylines long before she realized she was building the foundation of a writer.

As an adult, Hayzel continued creating characters, shaping many of their experiences from fragments of real life and emotional truths. Her imagination often plays like a series of stories within her mind's eye, a quality that has become the cornerstone of her storytelling style. Translating those vivid inner scenes onto the page became a natural extension of her creative journey.

As life evolved and experiences deepened, Hayzel realized she could take her storytelling further entering the world of erotica. With encouragement from friends and a fellow author, she presents *She Did It & He Liked It*, a powerful collection of ten short erotic stories. Each tale explores erotic tension through layered storylines designed to capture the imagination, stimulate thought, and leave a lasting impression.

Why erotica? Because erotica is a part of life—whether some choose to embrace it or not.

Hayzel invites readers to meet her imaginary friends (or are they?) who reside within the caverns of her mind. This series of short stories explores a wide range of erotic emotions. Doors are opened, boundaries are tested, and readers are taken on intimate voyages through the lives of these characters across ten provocative stories.

She Did It & He Liked It offers voyeuristic roller-coaster experiences of sexual arousal, love encounters, confessions of the heart, heartbreak, and compromise inviting readers to see the genre, and perhaps themselves, from a different perspective.

Everyone has a little more to expose.

Place yourself in these erotic situations—because *She Did It, He Liked It…* and you will too.

www.ingramcontent.com/pod-product-compliance
Lightning Source LLC
Chambersburg PA
CBHW061520020726
47502CB00006B/2154